Bodyguard

a Den of Thieves Novel

By Allison Cosgrove

Dear AJ
Love Youu
Bunches ♡

First edition March 2016

ISBN-13: 978-1530370047

To All The Brokenhearted,
May You Find A Way To Love Again.

Chapter 1

The sun was shining and the birds were chirping. Olivia was having brunch at her local cafe just like she did every Saturday morning. She liked sitting on the patio in the warmer months, watching the people come and go. It was a nice break from her hectic everyday as a county prosecutor.

She took a sip of her coffee just as tires screeched. Olivia's head snapped up in the direction of the sound. A dark black sedan had just finished turning the corner at the end of her street.

It picked up speed as it shot down the road towards where she was sitting on her front porch.

Then just as suddenly as it had started racing towards her, it started slowing down.

The passenger window rolled down and the muzzle of a gun appeared.

The next few seconds passed by as if they were hours. In nightmarish slow motion she watched the flash of gun going off, heard the pop-pop as it fired a second time and felt the air whoosh by as the bullets passed by her.

Someone was shooting at her!

Olivia's breath caught in her chest as she dove off of her chair to the ground as the pop-pop continued.

The bullets whizzed by her head, striking the chair where she sat. They didn't stop. They just kept coming.

Pop.

Pop.

The last one found its target. Her left shoulder felt like she had been punched. She gasped in the air that had been knocked out of her and screamed.

The fire engulfed her shoulder and shot down the side of her body. She lay down as close to the ground as she could and whimpered. She could hear sirens in the background.

One of the men yelled something to the other and the car suddenly picked up speed and shot off down the road.

She didn't move. She couldn't. The pain in her shoulder was so bad she could barely catch a breath. She lay there on the ground watching the pool of blood slowly growing beside her.

She listened to the sirens getting closer and prayed they would make it in time. She didn't want to die. Not like this. It hurt too much.

Bright lights flashed. Red and Blue. She closed her eyes. She was tired and the pain was getting to be too much.

"Over here! We have one down!" a woman's voice called out.

She could feel hands on her. She was so tired.

She closed her eyes.

"Stay with me. Stay with me." She could hear the woman's voice but it sounded so far away.

She tried to open her eyes; they were so heavy she didn't have the strength.

"Ma'am? Can you hear me? Ma'am--" the bodiless voice got further and further away with each word.

Then her world faded to black.

*****

Bo closed his eyes and took a deep breath. It was early morning at D.O.T. Recovery Services and he had the small weight room all to himself.

Just the way he liked it.

He started every morning the same way: into the

office before anyone else to use the weight room in peace and quiet.

Not that he didn't like working out with the others. Cat was always a good work out partner. She kept him in line and on target, but he was one who enjoyed his solitude. He needed to find his balance in the morning before the rest of the world took his attention and whisked him off again.

He opened his eyes and looked in the mirror that covered one of the walls. He was shirtless, tiny beads of sweat coated his torso. His muscles ached slightly but it was a good ache, one he looked forward to daily.

He had been working out for over an hour and he was finally ready to start his day. It was a good thing too; he could hear sounds coming from the main room of the office. Everyone was slowly filtering in for the day.

He opened his eyes again. It was time to start his day. He took another deep breath and turned around as the door to the weight room opened and Cat walked in.

"Good morning," Cat sang cheerfully, as she gave him a light pat on the shoulder, "Have a good weekend?"

"Decent." Weekends for him weren't any different than the rest of the week. He spent the weekends prepping for upcoming cases and going over their gear to make sure that it was all in top working order in case they needed it and working out at the gym.

"Let me guess. You did the same thing you do every other weekend?"

He nodded.

"Bo you really need to live it up a little. Enjoy the finer points in life."

"Like what?"

"Oh hell, I don't know. Come out for drinks with us on a Friday night or something. You know, meet other people." She threw her hands up in the air.
They'd had this conversation more than once in the past. He had tried to go out with the rest of the team, but in the end everyone went home with other people and he went home alone. He had no wish to meet new people and go through the awkward conversation, the pretenses and the unspoken promises.

None of it appealed to him in the least. Then there was the drinking. The others tended to drink a lot. He, however, did not. He might have a beer or two once in awhile, but never to the excess that his teammates did. He didn't understand it really – why anyone would willingly put himself or herself into a position to act like a fool and not be in complete control for some of the time.

That wasn't something that he had the inclination to participate in.

"We know that won't work, Cat. Why do you insist on trying to change the way I do things?"

"Well you just seem to be so lonely all the time. And you never do anything fun or exciting. It's just the same old routine." She gave an exasperated sigh.

"Maybe I like routine."

"Ugh! I give up," Cat said throwing her arms out. "The rest of the gang is on their way in, you might want to get cleaned up and get into the office."

"Something going on today?"

"Jake wants to meet with us about something. Not sure what but... you know Jake."

He nodded. Jake didn't like to be kept waiting, a stickler for being on time and organized. He liked progress.

All the things he himself appreciated. Seven and a half years in the military will do that to a man.

"See you in the main room," Cat said waving as she walked out of the room.

*****

"Good morning, everyone!" Jake said walking into the room and passing out fresh coffees as he went.

Bo watched as everyone dutifully accepted their coffees. He noted that while Sebastian had not arrived as yet, everyone else was there.

"You are looking mighty pleased with life this morning," Rudy observed, sitting down at his bank of computer monitors in the back of the room and bending down to boot up the towers.

"As opposed to what?" Jake asked eyeing Rudy.

"Well, l have noticed you've been under a lot of stress lately…" Rudy's voice trailed off and Bo could tell by the look on his face that he wished he hadn't spoken up at all.

"Really now?" Jake glanced around the room and the rest of the team either shrugged or turned away to avoid his eyes.

When he looked at Bo, Bo just shrugged his shoulders and offered,

"Jake, you have been a little on edge lately. It's not hard for us to see it."
"Hmph," Jake grumbled, taking a swing of his coffee before continuing, "Well, if I have seemed a little 'on edge', as you put it, or if I have crossed any lines with any of you I am sincerely sorry."

"Jake, look, we weren't trying to--" Bo started again, trying to smooth any ruffled feathers.

"No, no. It's fine really, it is." Jake held up his hand to silence Bo, "I completely understand everyone's concern. I have been a little off my game lately and for that I really am sorry and I do have a valid reason for being that way."

He paused to take another gulp of coffee and everyone waited for him to continue.

"The reason I've been stressing out is that the offers are not as full as they have been in recent months." He shrugged, "We haven't had a solid assignment that brought in real money in a long time."

"We had that thing with that woman and her ancient artifact thing--" Cat piped up.

"That was over a month ago, Cat."

"The LCPD has been keeping us busy for the last few weeks," Paul offered

"Yes, they have and thank God for that because otherwise none of us would have had a pay cheque at the end of the week."

"Really, Gracie?" Paul looked over at Gracie who was fighting with her papers at her desk, trying to stay out of the conversation.

"He is right. We're not broke. At least not yet. And really it is not something to truly worry about right now but at the same time, Jake is right," Gracie nodded as she spoke, her cats eye glasses sliding slowly down her nose as she continued, "The work we do for the LCPD, while it pays the bills to a point, is not enough to sustain us completely. We are slowly dipping into our buffer money. It will eventually cause a huge problem if we don't stop the slow bleed."

"Thank you, Gracie, for explaining it." Jake smiled at her before turning back to the rest of the group.

"Why didn't you tell us this earlier?" Paul asked.

"To be honest, while it bothered me to some degree, I also knew we would eventually pull out of it and get back on the right path again." Jake shrugged, "And to be quite truthful, I didn't want anyone else to have to worry about it. That's the job of the team leader: to worry about these things."

"Fair enough." Bo nodded. "I am pretty sure that any one of us here would have shouldered that worry alone."

Bo knew all too well what it meant to have to lead a team into situations unknown from his time in the military. Far too many times he would have given anything to have been able to speak freely with one of those soldiers under him about the dangers they were headed into but he had not wanted to burden any of his men with that worry. Nor had he wanted that subconscious fear to erode their abilities or their confidence.

He understood entirely why Jake had chosen not to inform the others.

"If that's the case then the reason you have been in a rather chipper mood today must mean that something has cropped up to improve our situation," Rudy brightened.

"Indeed something has." Jake grinned.

"Did we win the lotto last night?" Cat asked returning the grin.

"Not unless you were the one that bought the winning lotto ticket," Jake cracked back.

Bo took a deep breath again and finally sat down on

the edge of his desk. He could feel the tension that had been in the air moment before lifting rapidly. They had all been friends for years and it always made him uncomfortable when they were at odds with each other. It didn't happen often but when it did, it didn't sit right with him.

Since he had left the army, these people were the only family and friends he had, really.

"I thought you, being our fearless leader and all, would be the one who procured the winning ticket," Cat shot back, her eyes lit up at the playful banter. "Just goes to show you can't trust a man to do such a simple task."
Everyone burst into laughter.

"I do apologize for any inconvenience that not winning the lotto may have caused, but I just don't think it's in the cards right now."

"Do tell then, Jake," Paul said, sweeping his hand across the room. "We are all waiting on our fearless leader to tell us the good news."

"You know we do a lot of work for the LCPD and they trust us to take care of our end of things in a polite and professional manner. We have been asked to take care of a special project for them where they require the utmost delicacy and sensitivity on our part."

"I take it by your enthusiasm that this job also comes with a sizable paycheck along with the level of delicacy and sensitivity that you described," Rudy's eyebrows raised in curiosity

Neither could help but wonder what it could be that had gotten Jake so excited about a job with the LCPD after having just said that the money they ere already making wasn't quite enough to cover their expenses each week.

"Yes, it does that, my geeky friend."

"Are you going to tell us what we are going to be doing or are we just going to have to sit here and guess?" Cat said seriously. Gone was the joking tone from moments before.

That was one thing about her he truly liked: while she was one of the first to join in on some playful banter, she was a big believer in the idea but there was a time for work and a time for play.

Playtime was over for Cat. Bo didn't mind the shift, he was curious to see what Jake had going and eager to get started

"You guys remember Stan Brookshire from the homicide department? Well he contacted me yesterday with an offer I couldn't refuse." Jake looked at his watch; "Stan should be here in a few minutes so I'll leave it for him to explain it to you."

"Alright you've heard the man guys, get your paper and crayons and let's get organized to make sure we do this right," Paul ordered clapping his hands.

Bo continued to sit there, staring at Paul. Paul was a good guy but he was a Fed through and through. They had a goofy, almost cheerleader stout way of rallying the troops and it tended to get on his nerves sometimes. That and the fact that Bo was never one to take notes for anything so every inch of this time was committed to memory as it was related to him.

Paul passed Bo on the way to his own desk.

"That's right, you don't need to take notes." Paul smiled and patted him on the shoulder as he went by.

Bo continued to watch the others preparing themselves. A quick glance at the clock showed it was about five minutes to eight; he hoped that Stan would not be late like he had been in the past or it would be a long day.

"Wait, has anyone seen Sebastian?" Jake said, scanning the room before his eyes landed on Sebastian's empty desk.
"Nope. I don't think he's in yet," Rudy replied without looking up from his computer screen.

Jake muttered something under his breath and returned to what he had been doing.

Sebastian better hurry up or he had better have a really good explanation if he gets any later, Bo thought, looking at the clock again.

*****

Stan was almost half an hour later than he said he would be. It wasn't as late as Stan had been in the past but it was just enough to send Jake into a foul mood again. To make it even worse, Sebastian still had not shown up.

"Sorry I'm late," Stan started as he and his partner Jane entered. Bo could hear the rain hitting the pavement as the door opened and both were shaking off the raindrops. Gracie cringed as they did so; she liked a neat and orderly office. Bo remembered one time in particular when some of them had come in from a pretty messy assignment and had tracked in a whole pile of mud and Gracie had almost had a heart attack in the middle of the office. Gracie was biting her tongue right now but thankfully staying quiet.
 "I believe all of you have met my partner, Jane, "

Most of them had.

"Alright then, let's get down to business." Stan brushed his unkempt black hair off his forehead.

"Jake here tells us you have an interesting assignment for us," Paul said, motioning for Jane to follow him to the conference table in the middle of the room.

 "I do – I mean, I'm not sure that it's what you would call interesting but it certainly is one of the more important cases I have come across." He dropped the file in the middle of the conference table as everyone gathered around.

Stan opened the file; Bo could see a picture of a beautiful woman on the top of the stack of papers. Her dark eyes contrasted with her coffee colored skin. Her eyes held his gaze even from the photograph.

"Who is she?" Paul asked picking up the picture to have a better look before passing it around to everyone.

"She's Olivia Woods, the County prosecutor and a damn good one at that," Jane piped up.

"What's the deal with her?" Cat asked, peering at the picture closely before passing it to Bo. Olivia's eyes continued to stare back at him and he forced himself to look away. He studied the rest of her, from her perfectly coiffed hair to her neat black suit and white blouse, not a single hair seemed to be out of place on the woman.

"She missing or a convict or something?" he asked, taking the picture from Jane. "Funny but no. She was shot last week," Stan said, retrieving the picture. "What does that have to do with us?" Cat crossed her arms as she spoke.

"You want us to find the son of a bitch who did it?"

Paul assumed, clearly angry that the crime had been committed. Being a Fed, he was eminently protective of other branches and the attorneys that persecuted the criminals and saw to justice for the victims.

"Actually, I have something else in mind for you," Stan countered, looking around the table at the others.

Everyone waited for Stan to elaborate.

"What we need you to do is protect her until we can find out who attacked her," Jane explained.

No one said anything but looked around at each other.

"With all due respect, Stan, I understand that this is an important case, but we do not provide protective services; we are in the recovery business," Paul piped up first.

"Paul's right; we don't do protective services or anything even remotely close to that." Cat looked almost offended at the idea.

"Come on, guys," Jake said. "Let's hear what Stan and

Jane have to say before we jump to any conclusions about the job."

Bo's mind raced. He did not want anything to do with protecting anyone, let alone a woman. What the hell was Jake thinking, taking on an assignment like this?

"I don't know what --" Paul started and then stopped short when Jake raised his hand.

"Stan, go on." Jake nodded at Stan.

"Anyway, as I was saying. We need you to keep an eye on this woman for us."

"'We' being who?" Cat asked, eyeing Stan suspiciously.

"Me and Jane." Stan motioned towards Jane as he spoke.

"You and Jane. Does that mean what I think that means?" Paul looked between Jake and Stan.

Bo could feel the tension rising in the room.

"Yes. It means that this is not something that the LCPD is asking for but rather something that Jane and I are asking for. A favor, if you will."

"Great, just great. Now we're doing favors." Cat threw her hands up in the air as she turned away from the table.

"Easy, Cat," Jake warned.

"Seriously, Jake, no offense meant Detective Brookshire, but when did we start doing favors?"

"Since we have to." Jake's temper was visibly rising as Cat shook her head and walked into the next room.

"I apologize, Stan."

"No need." Stan held up his hand to silence Jake. "I get it. It's not something you do on a regular basis and that's why everyone is grumpy."

"'Grumpy' isn't quite the word I'd use for Cat," Rudy said, shaking his head.

"Well whatever we call it, we are taking the case." Jake leaned on the edge of the conference table.

"Know what, I get that you all have some things to

discuss, so we will leave you to it." Then he turned and Jane followed.

"I'll call you," Jake promised, walking Stan and Jane of the door.

Chapter 2

Jake followed the two detectives out of the room.

"Well, this is interesting," Rudy remarked, as soon as the door closed behind the trio.

"You can say that again," Cat agreed, joining the group. "Glad to see you coming back to the table, Cat," Paul welcomed, picking up the file and leafing through it.

"I'm only coming back because I want to talk to you guys about this and hopefully talk some sense into you."

"Great, now it's nonsense." Paul rolled his eyes. "Bo, you haven't said much this whole time - what do you think about the assignment? Is it really that bad?"

Bo didn't respond. He was trying to remain non-committal but he wasn't entirely on board with the assignment; it wasn't his ideal situation.

"See, even Bo thinks this assignment is a crock," Cat waved her hands in the air.

"Bo?" Paul raised his eyebrows, waiting.

"I'm not entirely sure that we, as a company, should start branching out into protective detail. We could be sitting setting ourselves up for some tough calls down the road that we might not want to make. Money is always going to be tight."

"See?" Cat waved her hand again before turning away.

"I didn't finish," he started again, pausing to wait until everyone was paying attention before continuing. "Given the scenario of the case and that the person asking is someone who not only provides us with a steady stream of revenue but also someone who has been there for us on a regular to back us up, I think we should take this case on if only to keep our relationship with the detectives strong."

"That is logical," Rudy agreed as Jake walked back into the room trailed, by a very disheveled looking Sebastian.

"Good of you to join us, Sebastian." Paul shook his head.

"Late night with Daria again?" chuckled Cat.

"Don't. Okay?" Sebastian grumbled

"Guys, leave the man be." Jake called everyone back to the table. "I brought Sebastian up to speed on where we are with this thing."

"So, it's settled then?" Cat crossed her arms clearly unimpressed.

"Yes, we are taking the case. And yes, everyone is going to help out as much as is needed."

"So who gets to play babysitter?" Sebastian piped up, putting down the picture of Olivia he had picked up a moment before.

"It sure isn't going to be me," Cat mumbled

"No Cat, it's not going to be you. Bo," Jake drew a breath, "is going to handle the client's safety. The rest of us will be there to support him and Stan's investigation in any way necessary."

Bo started to protest, "Why me?"

"Your military background makes you ideal for the job," Jake said, making notes on a sheet of paper from the file.

"But Jake, wouldn't Sebastian be better? His people skills are far better than mine." He had a feeling that he was fighting a losing battle.

He didn't want to be in charge of protecting anything or anyone.

"If we needed someone to seduce someone else, Sebastian would fit that bill. We need the best protection; you fit that bill."

"But Cat also fits that bill. She's got just as much skill as I--"

"Bo, that's enough. You're going to be the one who takes protective detail for Olivia Woods and that is final."

Cat snickered and Bo felt his irritation rise.

"Leave it alone, Cat," Bo growled and idly picked at the file on the table.

"I'll be cleaning and oiling gear if you need me," Cat smiled sweetly. "Good luck babysitting."

Bo glared at her as she left the room. As much as he appreciated her humor, it didn't always feel great to be on the receiving end of it.

"Alright, alright. Get your gear together, Bo and head over to the hospital," Jake ordered, handing Bo the slip of paper he had copied things on to. "Here is the room number."

"Thanks," he mumbled stuffing the paper in his pocket without looking at it.

*****

Olivia closed her eyes and rested her head back on the pillow. The pain coming and going in waves was emanating from her shoulder.

The painkillers they had given her earlier were starting to wear off, but as much as it was starting to hurt again, she didn't enjoy the funky feeling in her mind.

She needed to have all her faculties if she was going to figure out who was behind this.

Opening her eyes, she stared at the ceiling trying to fight back the tears. There was any number of people who could have wanted her dead. It was her job to prosecute any number of the negative elements that called Lake City their home. Any number them could want her dead. Finding out exactly who did this was going to take an extremely long amount of time and a lot of resources. Leaving whomever was behind it, time to come back and finish the job.

Tears built up in the corners of her eyes before making their way down her cheeks.

The door opened suddenly, snapping her out of it. She hurriedly wiped the tears away before the curtains around her bed parted and two people stepped in.

"Good afternoon. Olivia Woods?" The dark haired man started, reaching out his hand. "I'm Detective

Stan Brookshire and this here is my partner, Detective Jane Trinity."

"Detectives." She nodded then winced; the movement had caused the pain to radiate from her shoulder.

"Don't move, Miss Woods, we wouldn't want you to hurt yourself on account of us."

The woman, Jane, smiled warmly at her and she pulled out her notepad and pen.

"I know you two." Their faces were familiar but the lingering fog in her head was making it hard to focus.

"Yes, Miss Woods, we have probably met at some point in our careers." Detective Brookshire shuffled uncomfortably, "We need to go over a few things together."

Olivia nodded, her mind still trying to make the connection of how she knew them. It was frustrating to know that her mind wasn't up to the usual. She never forgot a face but the meds were clouding her mind.

"Miss Woods?" Detective Trinity was looking at her

intensely.

"I'm sorry, my mind was wandering a little bit." She tried to smile but it felt fake. "What was the question?"

"We are trying to think of a list of people that would want to hurt you or want you dead," Detective Brookshire repeated the question.

"To be quite honest, Detective, I was asking myself the same question as you were walking into my room."

"Did you come up with any names?" The man moved forward to the edge of his seat, listening.

"Detectives, I am Crown prosecutor. There is a list a mile long of people who would love to do me harm."

"Anyone that stands out as a prime suspect?"

"Not particularly."

"Has anyone made any threats against you or your office recently?" The detective Trinity asked, without looking up from the note she was making.

"You have to speak with my clerks, they would know better than I would."

"Do they handle your incoming mail?" he asked.

"Yes, most of it. The only time I would hear about something of that nature would be if there was an imminent threat to my safety." She sighed. "But I will tell you from what I understand there are any number of lunatics that have had their objections to my existence."

"Any particular reason that stands out?" The man smiled at her description of the situation.

"Because I dress too nicely, my house is too tidy. Because I put Big Brother, Little Sister, Mom. Daughter, Son, Father in jail. Because I drank my latte this morning from a disposable cup," she laughed quietly.

"So... nothing in particular."

"Not really any one thing, no. I'm sorry, Detective. I wish I was more help but truthfully I'm at a loss." She sighed heavily and went on, "Somehow I think this will be easier to come to terms with if I could understand the reason it happened in the first place."

"I wish I had an answer for you right now. We are still taking to some of the witnesses who were at the scene. For now, we don't think there is an immediate threat to your life."

"I noticed the guard standing outside my door, thank you for that."

"You're welcome, however, we do have a solution for you when you're ready to leave the hospital which from what the doctors have told me, could be any day now."

"Oh God. I hope you're not going to have one of those creepy undercover cops follow me around, are you?" She groaned outwardly. The very thought of someone following her around the city gave her the creeps. Not to mention how her family and friends would react to being followed wherever they went with her.

"No, Miss Woods, given that the police department's budget isn't what is supposed to be at, we can't spare as many Undercovers as we might have been able to in the past. The Justice Department is, however, able to take care of the bill for any expenses for whatever we decide. Besides that, any criminal worth his salt would be able to spot an unmarked car a mile away and find a way around it."

"Just what do you propose?" She eyed the detective suspiciously.

"We have a team of professionals who will be able to see to your protection."

"Professional bodyguards?" She inwardly groaned and rolled her eyes to the ceiling as she tried to sink deeper into her pillow.

She liked this idea even less than the unmarked undercover officer she'd just been refused. A bodyguard would be worse by far, they were allowed to go anywhere or do anything. Her freedoms would be even more limited.

"It's not forever, Miss Woods," the woman detective said soothingly, placing a hand on her shoulder.

"There is so much for me to do every day; how can I possibly get someone to run through the chaos with me?"

"We've spoken to the DA and he's modifying your schedule-" Stan started, and she could feel her blood pressure rising as she found herself tuning out the actual words he was speaking.

How dare he? Who did this man think he was?

"Stop. Just stop." She raised her right hand to silence him. "Miss Wood-" the other woman started, but she only had to flip her hand again in her direction to silence her too.

"Detectives, I understand you both have a job to do, and I understand that part of that includes ensuring that I am no longer in danger." She paused to catch her breath; the ache in her shoulders and head had increased to throbbing as her blood pressure had risen. "However, I too have a job to do and one that also includes making sure those responsible for doing things like this to me and others are thrown behind bars so they can't hurt anyone else. I cannot do my job if I am tethered to another person or anchored in one spot, unable to move for fear I might be hurt."

"We understand that, Ma'am and that is precisely why we opted for a twenty-four-hour bodyguard versus the city owned and operated security detail." Stan nodded as he spoke, "We had a feeling that you would not want to be stuck in one spot and unable to do things that are important to you."

"And what, you think an overgrown babysitter will do the trick?" She snorted. "You are kidding, right?"

The look on the man's face told her otherwise. He was not kidding.

"I am truly sorry but this isn't up for debate, Miss Woods," Jane told her softly.

Olivia bit back the tears; her shoulder started to throb again. Her anger at her own weakness became overwhelming and bile began rising up in her throat.

"I know it's not what you want to hear right-" the other woman started before Olivia cut her off.

"Really? Do you know? Do you understand what I'm going through?" She fired at the woman enough to make her jump.

Jane started to open her mouth but Olivia had had enough.

Allison Cosgrove | 40

"No, Detective. You. Don't. Know," she spat. "You have the training and the means to protect yourself while I am now going to have to rely on some rent-a-cop to follow me around."

She paused to catch her breath; neither detective made a move or uttered a word. They were waiting for her.

"And what is that going to look like to my peers? Or worse yet, to the criminals that I am set to prosecute? The only thing they are going to see is weakness. The defense attorneys are going to jump all over this like flies to shit."

"I get it, Miss Woods. But there is no other option for us. We have a duty to keep you safe and that is what we are intent on doing. I am sorry if that is not something you'd like to consider, but at this point, you have no choice," Stan said, rising.

His partner stood up, too.

"So that's it then?" Olivia huffed.

"For now," the man replied.

"Why, what else have you up your sleeve?"

"I will want to discuss the events of that morning but not today. You need your rest." He smiled.

She could tell he was really trying to be fair but she wasn't ready to admit defeat yet.

"Fine then," she mumbled as the detectives walked out of the room.

As the door shut behind them, the floodgates opened and she started to cry.

*****

Bo grabbed his bag as he stormed out of D.O.T.. He had spent the last ten minutes in his jeep going over each of the items in his pack.

He never left base without double-checking his gear. He never wanted to be in a situation where he didn't have what he needed.

He had been there once before and it had cost him dearly. He wasn't about to allow himself to be in that vulnerable position again any time soon. Not if he could help it anyway.

Putting the car into reverse, he backed out of his spot and started to make his way downtown to the hospital, silently cursing the rest of the team for foisting this on him in the first place. He did not want to be protecting anyone.

That wasn't what he had signed up for.

His phone rang and he glanced down at it before he accepted the call.

"Yes, Cat," he spoke.

"Hi Bo," Cat's voice came through the car's speakers.

"What would you like, Cat?" He turned onto the main highway.

"I just wanted to see how you were doing."

"Really? Seemed like you were of the same opinion as everyone else in there just a few short minutes ago."

"Yeah, about that--" she started and then trailed off.

"Don't worry about it, Cat."

"I am sorry, Bo. I guess I just got carried away in the moment like everyone else." She really did sound sincere.

She had, after all, called to make sure he was okay.

"It's fine, Cat, really., he sighed as he responded. He really didn't have the heart to be mad at his best friend.

"No, it isn't alright, Bo. They shouldn't be putting you in a situation where you are not comfortable. It's really not fair."

"Well, maybe they are right this time. Maybe it is time I put the past in the past and moved on with things. I mean, there isn't a way for me to change the past so I might as well let it go."

"Everyone deals with things in different ways, Bo. You have to deal with your things in the way or ways that make sense to you. If you aren't ready for something like this, there should be no one out there who will force you to be ready when you aren't." He could hear the concern in her voice.

"I am fine, Cat, really I am."

"If you aren't up to it, Bo, I will just tell Paul and Jake that I will do it. You don't have to. Really."

"Cat." He knew she was only trying to help him but at the same time he was starting to think that maybe it was time for him to move on and let the past stay in the past where it belonged.

"If you're sure, Bo."

"Yes, I am sure, Cat."

"You will tell me if it turns out to be too much for you, right?"

"I promise that you will be the first person I call."

"Alright. I am going to hold you to that, you know. There will be no escaping me if you start going off the rails and you don't ask for help."

"I am not going to go off the rails, Cat. You don't need to worry quite as much as you are doing right at the moment."

"Fine, if you say so."

"I do."

"Alright, I will check in with you later then."

"I look forward to it." A smile crossed his face. No matter what hell went on around him, he could always take comfort in the friendship he had with Cat.

He drove through the streets, wishing somehow she was going to be there with him. Not that he needed the support to do the job, but she was one of the few people who understood that even though the job came first, there were some things that even he had a hard time dealing with.

Some things just brought back too many memories for him and made the job very difficult. Though they had not talked much about their pasts, he knew that she too harbored the same guilt and scars that he did. That they had gone in to do a job and they were the ones who had ended up damaged in some way. A way that would never completely heal.

He shook his head and tried to clear away the

dangerous thoughts that invaded his mind. He did not need them to surface now. Now he needed to focus on the task at hand.

Bo turned off the highway onto the off ramp and headed into the heart of the city towards the hospital.

He wondered what she was going to be like. She seemed like the strong, independent type. The file stated that she was one of the top prosecutors in the country and had one of the highest conviction rates around. That in itself would make a whole lot of the criminals that existed in every city very unhappy that she was around.

It would make them happier still to know that she had been hurt and that would possibly give them a chance to finish her off in her weakened state.

That was something that he was not about to allow. He had spent many years on protective detail in the army, protecting civilians and dignitaries alike. Even when he had come back home, he had continued to do the odd protection job until eventually the demons of his past had caught up to him and he found he could no longer do that line of work.

That was when he had hooked up with the group at D.O.T.. It had been right up his alley. Just enough action that he didn't get bored but no one other than his team had needed his protection.

Until now.

He only hoped that he would be able to live up to the job and not let the rest of the team down.

Chapter 3

Bo took a deep breath and got out of his Jeep. The wind picked up as he closed the door, sending a few leaves and a paper coffee cup bouncing across the parking lot.

He pulled his jacket close and took a quick glance at the sky. The weather report said it might rain later on. Bo doubted the sky would hold another hour the way the clouds are gathering.

Crossing the parking lot, he nodded to the security guard that was under the hospital.

"Morning, Sir," the man waved to him. "Morning." Bo turned back and moved on.

Bo hated hospitals. They were wonderful as far as the advances in medicine and the seemingly miraculous things they could do nowadays. However, woeful moans and sharp cries of agony brought back memories of his time in the war. He could still see the faces of the innocent victims caught up in a battle that wasn't their choice to fight. He remembered the mothers wailing over their dead husbands' bodies, others begging him to take their child with him back to the Western world where things were safer. The look in their eyes was burned into his mind forever.

"Are you going up?" the petite blonde asked, holding the elevator door open for him, smiling.

"Yes. Sorry." He cleared his throat, which had suddenly become dry.

The door closed behind him as he stepped on and pushed the button for the fifth floor.

"Family?" The woman spoke again as the elevator begin to move upwards.

"No," he answered a little too sharply and immediately felt bad about it.

"Oh. Sorry," she mumbled, the friendly light in her blue eyes fading as she looked down at her shoes.

"No, I'm sorry I was rude," he mumbled, feeling awkward. "I'm here to see a friend but I'm afraid I don't like hospitals that much."

"I'm not sure there is anyone who really likes hospitals." Her face brightening again, "Well, maybe the doctors and nurses do at to some extent. I mean, they get to make people feel better and stuff."

Bo looked at her a moment, saying nothing, as the elevator arrived on his floor and he stepped out.

"Have a nice day." She beamed. "Well, as good as you can have."

"You too," he mumbled and headed off down the hallway as the doors closed once again.

Scanning the hallway, he could see two uniformed officers talking to each other at the end of the hall. He took a deep breath to re-center his mind before he approached them. He had a job to do and no good would come of him failing to be completely on point.

"Good afternoon, officers." Bo nodded at them as he came up in front of them.

Bo noticed they both instinctively placed their hands on the butts of their guns.

"Can we help you?" the taller one asked.

"I'm here to see Miss Wood---" Bo started to reply.

"Miss Woods is not receiving visitors at this time," the other man cut him off, his hand still on his weapon.

"I understand that but I'll try it again---"

"Look, we don't want any trouble here, pal, so unless you're family, you would do best to move along."

"Honestly, officers, I'm not looking for trouble---"

"Good. Then we'll be moving along then?"

The back and forth with these two was making his

head spin. The constant interrupting was irritating him. It was not a good combination.

"Officers, while I understand that you are both just doing your job, if you would be ever so kind as to let me finish what I was saying, you would see that I do have a legitimate reason for being here," Bo grumbled, trying to keep his temper from overflowing.

"Really, and just what would that be?" the tall one sneered.

"I've been asked to come here by Detective Stan Brookshire. The company I work for has been hired to protect Miss Woods upon her release from the hospital."

The two uniforms looked at each other and then back at Bo.

"What is the name of the company that you work for? Shorty, I.D. him again," relaxing a little.

"D.O.T. Recovery."

"Recovery company?" The tension was back in a blink of an eye.

"Listen." Bo held up his hands. "We are a recovery company, yes, but we are helping Miss Woods as a favor to Detective Brookshire."

"Sure you are." Suspicion and leeriness seeping into this voice, "Are you with the press?" Tallboy glared at him as Shorty turned away and spoke into his radio.

"I completely understand where you guys are coming from. I wouldn't trust anyone either, given the circumstances. You guys are doing your jobs same as I am." Bo took a deep breath, reminding himself that the officers, while slightly annoying, were only doing their jobs. "Once your partner confirms what I've told you, you will see."

His partner did not take his eyes off Bo. Minutes dragged on for what seemed like hours before Shorty returned to them and smiled.

"He's clear."

Tallboy nodded and visibly relaxed his shoulders.

"We are very sorry about that." Shorty reached out his hand to Bo, "I'm Tom Glavine and this here is Joe

King."

"Bo Jackson," Bo reciprocated, shaking both men's hands.

"Like that football player?" Tom asked, smiling.

"Something like that." Bo groaned inwardly. If he had a dollar for every time someone made that comment, he would never have to work another day in his life.

"Anything we can do to help you?" Joe offered.

"Nothing at the moment, but I'll speak to you once I've had the chance to introduce myself to Miss Woods."

"Of course," Jim said, suddenly cheery and stepping aside to allow Bo to enter the room.

He stepped into her room; the first bed just inside the door was empty. The curtains were drawn on the bed closest to the window.

"Miss Woods?" Bo said, stepping up to the wrong person.

"Who is it?" a woman's voice replied quietly.

"My name is Bo Jackson, Ma'am. I'm from the D.O.T.; Detective Brookshire sent me." Bo figured it was best to get it all out at once after his little run in with the officers out front.

He waited for her to reply.

"Now, if this is a bad time, I can come back a little later."

He could hear her sigh before she spoke.

"I would rather you just not come back at all, but I highly doubt that is going to happen."

"I am sorry, Ma'am, but we both know that isn't going to happen."

"I know," the disembodied voice replied.

Bo waited.

"You might as well come in since I can't get rid of you."

"Thank you, Ma'am," Bo said, parting the curtains and stepping inside.

He stopped. The picture they have been given had depicted a beautiful, strong-looking prosecutor, the kind of woman who cut you down with a glance.

The woman lying in the hospital bed shared the same high cheekbones and the plump lips, but gone was the perfectly dyed hair and the tough as nails stature.

She looked so helpless lying there, hooked up to I.V.s and monitors.

"What? You act like you've never seen a woman lying in a hospital bed before." While her body might have been temporarily rendered helpless, there was no missing the fire in her brown eyes.

"My apologies, Ma'am," Bo mumbled, momentarily losing his train of thought.

"Mr. Jackson, We are going to be spending a lot of time together in the coming weeks, correct?"

"Yes, as far as I'm aware, I will be with you until either they catch the person or the persons responsible, or until they believe the threat on your life has been neutralized."

"Whatever," she waved her hand, "And since we are going to be spending time together, there is one thing that you're going to have to do for me immediately."

"Of course, what would you like?" He was confused briefly, but felt slightly curious as to what her request would be.

"You really need to stop calling me 'ma'am'."

*****

Olivia stared at him. He was a good-looking man. Clearly he spent a lot of time at the gym, based on his well-chiseled figure.

"Excuse me?" His deep brown eyes looked perplexed.

"I said that you are going to have to stop calling me ma'am if we are going to spend the next little while together."

"Okay. Miss Woods---" he started again before she cut him off.

"Please, Olivia." She held up her good hand, wincing slightly as she shifted, causing a sharp pain in her bad shoulder.

"Olivia," he repeated and stood there looking uncomfortable.

"Have a seat, you look absolutely ridiculous standing there, looking like that."

He dutifully sat in the chair that the detective had been sitting in a short while before.

"So," she said to him, "Are we just going to sit here in silence or do you have things you need to talk to me about?"

"Yes, I'm sorry I---"

"I get it. From what I've learned in the last ten minutes, being someone's bodyguard isn't exactly what you signed up to do."

He looked at her confused again.

"Good ears. I could hear you getting through the good

old boys out there."

He smiled.

"Good you *are* human." She smiled back.

"Yes. We should discuss the plan for when you are discharged from the hospital."

She nodded and let out a sigh. She was hoping that whatever was going on was over and dealt with before the doctor thought about releasing her. She wanted to get back to work.

"Ma'am?" His smooth voice cut through her thoughts.

"Olivia," she said absently, thinking about what she needed to get done once she got herself back to the office. Her mind was not on whatever it was he was talking to her about.

"Did you hear what I said?"

"No, I'm sorry, what did you say your name was again?"

"Bo Jackson, Ma--- Olivia."

"Bo. Good." She would have to try to remember that.

"Please don't say anything about being related to the football player." His face was serious but she could see a small twinkle in his eye.

Maybe this won't be so bad, she thought.

"What were you saying, Bo?" she asked, pulling her mind back to the task at hand.

"I was asking if you knew when they were thinking of letting you out of here?"

"I don't know. They haven't said. Although, if I had my way, it would be sooner rather than later."

He nodded, "I understand."

She looked at him, trying to make out what he was all about. *Quiet* was the first word that came to mind. *Brooding* was another. She wondered what sort of a man would make recovery work his job.

"So," she started in an effort to restart the conversation. The man was certainly not much of a conversationalist.

"We need to find out when they are letting you out. As soon as you know, you will have to make sure you let me or one of the other members of D.O.T. know."

"You're not going to be the one watching me the entire time?" She was sure the detective had said that there would be one bodyguard at all times.

A slight tremor in her stomach began. If there were more of them, how was she going to be able to tell them all from one another? How would she distinguish the people sent to protect her from the people who might come to do her harm?

"I am going to be the one with you most, if not all of the time. I only meant that if I was out taking care of things for your return home, and I was unreachable that you would be able to contact my associates in the meantime."

"For a second there, I thought that I was going to have to deal with more than one of you."

"I can assure you, one of us is more than enough."

"You said that you are from D.O.T. Recovery. What sort of recovery is that, that would need that sort of specialty?" she asked, finally finding her way into the line of questions she wanted to ask.

"We find things that people need finding, Ma'am."

"What sorts of things would need finding that would employ people who could double as a bodyguard?" she pressed.

"Sometimes things are taken by people who are less than scrupulous and we have to retrieve them and get them back to their rightful owners," he explained, looking at his hands.

She watched him rub his hands together. His fingers long, his palms had a slight callous to them. Definitely a man who used the weight room at the local gym.

"Sort of like pirates?" she asked quietly, still watching his fingers move slowly back and forth together.

"Hmm?" he asked looking up, their eyes met. Her breath caught in her throat, as their eyes locked for a moment.

"The people you have to track down, they are sort of like pirates?" She looked away at her own hands, immediately starting to pick at the tape on her I.V.

"Something like that, I guess you could say." He was still looking at her. She could feel the heat of his gaze.

What was he looking at? Surely she wasn't anything to look at in the condition she was in at that moment.

"Is it dangerous?" she asked, returning his gaze, hoping to make him look away, but he held her eyes.

"Sometimes."

She nodded and looked away again. Her mind was all fuzzy and she blamed the drugs that they had her on for the pain. It made her angry that she had so little control over her mind. She was not used to being out of control.

"So, what do you do?" she asked, not looking up again, but fighting to keep him talking so she would have time to clear her head of some of the fog.

"What do you mean?"

"I mean for the company. What is your roll? Or are you simply just the hired gun?"

He laughed.

"You have a very odd perception of the way our company works."

"Well, you just said that you are in a recovery business and that you fight against pirates, and that sometimes it gets dangerous."

"I suppose I did, but how did you get that I am, as you called it, 'a hired gun' out of that?" His eyebrow raised in curiosity.

"You are the one your boss sent to be my bodyguard, so I would have to assume that you are the one with the most skill and experience in protecting someone from danger."

He didn't say anything for a moment, she wondered if she had made him angry. Not that it really should have mattered to her, she honestly didn't want him there in the first place, but there was something about him that had managed to disarm some of the hostility she'd originally had towards the idea.

That was one of her biggest weaknesses. Inside the courtroom, she was strong and almost ruthless with her job, there wasn't anything she wasn't willing to do to make sure that justice for the victims was had. But the second she stepped out of the courtroom, away from her office, she had this soft side to her that left her feeling incredibly vulnerable.

"I guess that is true," he said abruptly.

"I'm sorry. I didn't mean to pry," she apologized, realizing she might struck a nerve.

"Don't worry about it. I really should get going," he said, standing up. "I would like to head over to your apartment and have a look around and make sure it is safe and secure for you there."

"Yes, of course." She swallowed hard, his short tone striking at her already frayed nerves. "My keys are in drawer there."

She motioned with her good hand to the side table.

He reached in and scooped her keys out.

"You really shouldn't leave them so readily accessible when there is a threat on your life." He glared at her.

"Well I didn't think anyone would be so interested in my keys if they were able to get past the armed guards at my door." She glared back; if he was going to be like that, two could play at that game.

He turned and started out of the room.

"What, no goodbye?" she snapped at his back.

He turned around and gave her a look before leaving without saying a word.

*****

Bo stormed out of Olivia's room. What the hell was he thinking? There was no way that he was going to be able to do this. Cat was right. He wasn't ready for this and he might never be ready.

"Everything alright?" Tim asked, as he left the room.

"Fine. Just going to head over to Miss Woods' house now and make sure things are ready for her to come home."

"She going home soon?" Joe asked.

"Not that I know of, but knowing my luck I'll be the last to hear about it when it happens. The lady doesn't like the idea of having a bodyguard."

"Yeah, she does seem to be a bit on the feisty side," Tim chuckled.

"Yeah," Bo agreed. He wished he could get out of the hospital that moment but if he left too quickly, the cops might say something to Detective Brookshire and then he would never hear the end of it from Jake.

"If you need us please let us know," Joe observed, "You seem to need to get on your way."

"Yes, thank you." Bo nodded and made his way back down the hall to the elevators. He could still feel the watchful eyes of the officers on him as he boarded the elevator.

In the elevator, he replayed the entire encounter with Olivia Woods. While she seemed helpless, she clearly wasn't entirely. There was still quite a bit of spunk in her and she clearly was not going to be an easy asset to protect.

Not to mention, she asked too many questions. All of the others he had protected over the years had just let him do his job and not bothered with idle chatter, but this woman asked questions like he was a witness on the stand. Questions that he did not feel like answering.

Why he had agreed to this assignment against everything his mind was telling him was beyond his understanding.

He shook his head and got off the elevator.

After making his way through the pouring rain, he got into his jeep and took a deep breath before putting the key in the ignition. He was going to have to find a way to explain to Jake that there was no way that he was going to be able to continue with the assignment.

By the time he had made it back to D.O.T., he had almost come up with the words that he was going to say to Jake. He didn't so much care about what the others thought, as it wasn't up to them. Cat would no doubt back him up, but really he didn't care what else happened.

He walked into the office and scanned the room for Jake.

"What's wrong, Bo?" Gracie asked, standing up from her desk and moving to meet him as he went by.

"Jake around?" he asked.

"Right here," Jake said, popping his head out from the weight room. "What's up?"

"We need to talk," Bo said, ushering Jake back in the weight room.

Once they were inside the door, Bo closed the door behind them and turned around to face Jake, taking a deep breath as he went.

"Bo, what in the hell is going on?"

"I can't do this." The speech he had thought about the entire ride back to the office suddenly evaporated.

"Do what?" Jake looked confused, and really Bo couldn't blame him.

"Be a bodyguard. I can't do it, Jake." The words were coming out but they sounded like they were coming from someone else.

"Bo, I don't know what the hell is going on, but you aren't making a whole shitload of sense at the moment."

Bo rubbed his face.

"Jake, I cannot be the person in charge of ensuring the safety of Olivia Woods."

"Bo, I am really not sure what in the hell that has come over you but you have to understand that there is no other option. This is your assignment and you have to see it through to the end." Jake folded his arms across his chest.

"I cant do it."

"Yes, I have heard you say that three times now, but you still haven't told me why you cant do it."

"I am not ready to do this sort of thing again. Cat was right. I need more time." Bo didn't like the way he sounded.

Jake took a deep breath and sat down on the weight bench in the middle of the room. He rubbed his hands over his face and through his hair before he spoke.

"Look, Bo. We have known each other for a really long time. I backed you up on all sorts of different things and in so many different situations, but honestly as your friend, let alone your boss, I have to tell you that you have to pick up and move on. I know what you went through is nothing easy to have to deal with, but you can't keep hiding yourself from life just because you could end up in a similar situation. You have to pull your shit together, man," Jake advised, giving Bo a hard stare, "Besides, out of all of us, there really isn't any one of us that could do it better than you."

Bo looked around the room not wanting to look at Jake. He knew the man was only being logical and he really couldn't fault the guy.

"Jake..." his voice trailed away as he tried to come up with some sort of explanation or reason, all of the ones that he come up with on the way back to D.O.T. either sounded stupid now or if there was a brilliant gem in the pile, he had forgotten which it was.

"No, I am sorry to say this, but I am not changing my mind on this at all. Time to come back to the real world once again, my friend. The first one is always the toughest, so don't worry." Jake stood up and patted him on the shoulder. "You can come and talk to me any time if you need to. I am not going to abandon you, but you need to start standing up and dealing with things instead of running from them."

Jake turned and walked out of the room, leaving Bo standing there, wondering how he was going to handle the coming days.

Chapter 4

Bo didn't feel much like talking to anyone when he finally left the weight room. He spoke not a word to anyone as he crossed the main room, but he could tell that almost everyone was watching him.

What the hell were they thinking? His mind wandered, not that he cared that much what others thought, but he also didn't want them to start doubting his ability to perform his job. There was a distinct difference between him not feeling comfortable doing his job and him not being a capable of doing his job.

Not that anyone would really make that distinction and he knew it.

"You alright?" Cat asked, following him into the armory.

"I will be, if only because I have to be."

"What did I tell you, Bo? Jake can't make you do anything you don't want to do."

"I know what you said, Cat, but the man is my boss and I have to do as I am told." Bo pulled a case of monitoring equipment off the shelf and opened it to inspect it.

"Yes, you're right; he is your boss but he is also your friend. You need to sit down and have a talk with him about what you are going through and see if there is another way. I don't want you to be second guessing yourself in the field." She frowned, "It is that second guessing of ourselves that gets people like us hurt or worse."

"Cat." He stopped and wrapped his arm around her

shoulder, "I am going to be just fine. I know what I am doing, and I know that everything is going to turn out the way that it has to be in the end."

Cat leaned her head on his shoulder.

"Besides, maybe Jake is right, maybe I do need to stop wallowing in the past and get myself back on track."

"I hope you are right about that. If anything happened to…"

"Cat, no more of that, alright? Nothing is going to happen to me. I am only going to be babysitting the poor woman until they catch the bastard that fired on her."

"Fine, but Jake will suffer if anything---"

"Enough," Bo interrupted firmly and Cat pulled away.

"Since you wont let me talk you out of doing this because you are clearly a macho jerk today, at least you could let me help you pick out the toys and goodies that you are going to be needing for your assignment."

"Fine, fair enough, since I am being a macho jerk." Bo suddenly felt a weight lift off his shoulder.

As tough as this assignment was going to be, it would have been infinitely that much more difficult had he had to do it with the disapproving eye of his best friend watching over him.

"So, monitoring system: are you going audio and visual or straight visual?"

"Any reason you think I should use audio?"

"You never know, these bastards could see you coming and stay just out of camera range, but they would never know if there was super high grade microphone as well and that you would be able to hear them breath."

"Not sure that these guys are the type of folks who would worry about getting caught. Something about the whole drive-by shooting of a high ranking court official in the middle of the day tells me that they might not give a shit about being all stealthy."

"You might have a point there." Cat shrugged and made her way over to the bank of weapons on the wall.

"I'm thinking a few small hand guns, shotgun maybe?" he suggested as he watched Cat dance her fingers along the wall of firearms.

"I am thinking you might want to pack a little more heat than that. These guys weren't afraid to use a semi-automatic weapon in broad daylight. You should at least have something that can match that."

"Point taken. Just trying to avoid an all out firefight."

"Granted. Just take something along with you just in case."

Bo packed up the rest of the gear he figured he would need. Cat helped move it to the jeep without saying a word.

"You sure about this, Partner?" she asked once everything was carefully loaded in.

"Cat, I'm alright. Maybe Jake is right. Maybe it is time for me to break out of this and get back into the game the way I was trained."

"If you're sure --"

"I'm sure," he insisted, getting into the jeep and closing the door behind him.

As he pulled away from D.O.T., he glanced in the rearview mirror. Cat was still standing, watching him drive off. He could see her concern for him etched in the lines on her face. He knew he hadn't sounded as convincing as he had hoped.

Truthfully, he wasn't sure about anything other than he had a job to do.

The drive to Olivia's condo was uneventful and the traffic was light so it didn't take long to make his way across the city.

A doorman greeted him as he entered the front doors.

"Can I help you, Sir?" The older man looked at him suspiciously.

"Yes. I am here for Ms. Woods. I'm sure by now you've heard what's happened. I'll be looking after her to ensure her safety until the situation has been resolved."

The older man looked at him a moment before speaking.

"We had some detectives in here already this morning, asking questions."

"I know. They are the ones who hired the company I work for to handle Ms. Woods' security."

"You work for a security company?" The man's voice sounded a little more at ease but there was still a hint of suspicion in his voice.

"Give them a call if it will make you feel better about my being here. I don't mind waiting until you have confirmed with them that I have a legitimate reason for being here." Bo placed his gear on the ground at his feet.

"I'll do that. You just wait right there." The old man shuffled off slowly.

"Not going anywhere. Take your time," Bo assured him, watching him go, wondering how he was still standing. The man looked about ninety.

A minute later, Bo's cell phone started ringing.

"Jackson," he answered it.

"You sure are causing a lot of shit, aren't you?" the voice on the other end of the line responded.

"I'm sorry?" He tried to place the voice, "Who is this?"

"Detective Brookshire."

"Oh." He had to smile, the man was certainly living up to his reputation, "Detective, I am sorry for the mess of phone calls you have had to field, I'm sure you're dealing with enough as it is."

"It's fine, Bo, at the end of the day I know D.O.T. is on the job. I think I would be more concerned if I wasn't hearing you lot making your way around the city, taking care of Ms. Woods."

"You never need to worry. We are on the job."

"Jane is talking to the doorman right now clearing everything up for you. Anything else you can think of off the top of your head that you will need? Things that I can maybe take care of ahead of time for you?"

"Not at the moment. But if I do, I'll give you a call?"

"No problem, you have my number, let me know what you need."

Bo was just hanging up when the doorman shuffled back.

"I'll take you up to her floor."

"Do you have a key, or do you need me to get one for you?" he asked as they headed towards the elevator.

"I already have one from Ms. Woods," he said, holding up Olivia's key ring.

The elevator door opened on Olivia's floor and the doorman lead the way down the long hall, to the north end of the building. Olivia's apartment was the door at the very end of the hallway.

The doorman unlocked the door for Bo before swinging the door open and ushering Bo inside.

Bo stepped into the apartment; everything in was neat

and in its place. It was the apartment of a highly organized individual. He had expected nothing less, given what he knew about Olivia.

"Do you need anything else from me?"

"No, I think I am good for now. I have some things I'll need to set up in the common areas but I'll let you know when I do that."

"No problem. I'll leave you to it then. You know where to find me when you need me." The old man waved a wrinkled hand over his shoulder as he turned and closed the door behind him.

Bo heard the lock click as his guide locked the door behind him.

Taking a deep breath, he turned back around to the task at hand and started unpacking his gear.

*****

The sun was shining. Olivia could feel the heat of it on her face as she brought her coffee cup up to her mouth. Taking a deep breath in through her nose, she inhaled the robust aroma of a well-roasted brew.

A blue jay called in the distance, barley audible above the hum of traffic on the road and the din of conversation as she sat, enjoying a quiet moment.

It had been a long week; her cases, while going well, felt like they were piling up lately. There seemed to be a never-ending river of hate and evil peppered with the crimes of the desperate and lost. As saddening as it was, she found her passion in seeing justice done, or at least as much as she could.

She picked up the newspaper and her croissant in the other hand. The headlines screamed for justice.

Sighing, she put the paper back down and sat watching the people coming and going. She often wondered about their lives. She'd look at what they were wearing or carrying and then hypothesize about where they might be coming from or headed to. There were some she saw every week but some were new and different.

She was just watching a young woman in sweats carrying a rolled up yoga mat when she heard the screech of tires.

She looked up and saw the car bearing down on her.

Her heart raced.

She watched, frozen, unable to move a muscle, as the car raced faster towards her.

In slow motion, the window on the rear passenger side of the car rolled down.

Her breath caught in her throat. She knew what was coming next. She tried to move but it was like her body had become fused to her chair.

She watched in horror as the muzzle of a gun slowly inched its way out the window.

She struggled against the invisible force holding her down, the panic sweeping over her swallowing up an any rational thoughts.

She watched, terrified, as the muzzle flashed right in front of her.

In sickening slow motion, she watched as the bullet moved towards her. She tried to move but found that she was still stuck to the chair.

The panic built up inside of her as the bullet moved closer. She struggled harder, terror washing over her in waves.

She felt the cold, sharp pain as the bullet hit her hard in the chest. She flew backwards, suddenly no longer stuck to her chair.

A scream rose up in her throat and all the pain and terror came tumbling out.

Blackness engulfed her as she continued to fall backwards.

"Miss Woods!" the voice called sharply.

Her eyes snapped open, the scream dying on her lips as reality came rushing back.

The room quickly flashed into focus as she clawed at the person who was suddenly at her bedside.

"Are you alright?" the young nurse asked, her eyes wide with fear.

"Water," Olivia croaked her throat dry and raw.

The nurse brought the straw up to her lips and she quickly sipped the cool water. Her throat instantly felt better.

"Feel better?" she asked, pulling the straw away from Olivia's mouth.

"I think so." The pain in her shoulder was the only thing sore and even that was only a dull throb.

"You were having a nightmare." The woman nodded relieved.

"Thank goodness that was all it was. It was so horrible." Olivia tried to shake the last of the terror from her mind.

"No doubt, but from what I understand it is completely normal, given what you have been through," she commented, smoothing Olivia's hair back off her forehead.

Olivia said nothing. She did not want this to be her normal. Not now or ever.

"Listen, I'll have the doctor come and visit you and see

if there isn't something he can give you that will help you sleep better." The warm smile that was meant to make Olivia feel better fell short of its mark, and faded quickly when Olivia didn't reciprocate in kind. "You need to get a good night's rest so you can heal faster."

Olivia nodded and the nurse left.

Once she had left and Olivia heard the door close, she allowed herself to sink back into her pillow, letting out a heavy gasp. The tears flowed freely, seconds later.

Big, heaving sobs shook her body, making the pain in her shoulder flare up. She couldn't stop and the pain in her shoulder only made her cry harder.

She didn't want to be here anymore, she just wanted to go home. She wanted her own bed, her own clothes. She didn't want to be around anyone else.

The sobs slowed to quiet hiccups as she lay there, waiting for the throbbing in her shoulder to subside.

Get a hold of yourself, she told herself, wishing she hadn't allowed her emotions to get the best of her.

"Miss Woods?" a man's voice called quietly.

"Yes?" she replied, quickly wiping her eyes with her good hand.

"How are you doing?" A young doctor stepped in between the curtains.

"As well as I can," she mumbled trying to compose herself as she spoke.

"Don't worry," he said softly, placing a hand on her good shoulder.

"I'm sorry?" She was confused; don't worry about what?

"You don't have to keep up your reputation with me. I know you're in pain and I know you aren't sleeping well."

She looked at him but said nothing. What was he trying to say?

"Look, I know you're having problems coming to terms with what has happened to--"

"I'm fine. I just really want to go home," she cut him

off. She had no inclination for his patronization.

"I understand."

"No, I don't think you do; I really need to get home."

He looked at her for a moment, saying nothing. She could see he was thinking through what he needed to say to her. She hoped it wasn't going to be more bad news. She didn't need any more of that any time soon.

"Look, Miss Woods. Being here at the hospital, we have the means to keep a medical eye on you, not that I believe that there are going to be any further complications, but you just never know with these things." He took a deep breath before continuing, "Also, here at the hospital, we have the means to keep you safer from those that would seek to do you harm. We have the ability to set up a security detail to make sure that no one gets near you that shouldn't."

"I already have a security detail for when I get home. I have a bodyguard who will be going everywhere with me once I am out."

"First off, there is nowhere out there that you need to be right now. Right now, you need your rest. Period."

Her jaw dropped. She did not like being told what she could and could not do. If this doctor was trying to win her over, trying to make her feel better, then he was going about it the wrong way.

"I understand that I need to rest, Doctor, but I also have a life. I can't be held in here indefinitely. Eventually, I am going to have to be let out to make room for someone else who needs this bed more than I do."

"I agree with you on that one, Miss Woods. I am only concerned about your safety. I would rather hold onto you as long as I can, than to let you back out there and have you come back with another hole in you."

She looked at him, his face creased with worry. Her heart softened a bit. The guy genuinely cared about what happened to his patients.

"I understand what you're saying, Doctor. I am just tired of being stuck here."

"I know. I completely understand that." He sighed, "Look, while I could clear you, medically, to go home now, can I talk you into staying one more night? That will give the police more time. Then, hopefully they will have tracked down the people responsible and I will feel better knowing you're going home safely."

She looked at him. He did mean well. And he was right. One more night wouldn't be so bad and they might catch the bastards. That would mean she wouldn't have to have a bodyguard and she could just go home in peace and get on with her life.

It seemed like a fair trade.

"Alright. I will behave myself and stay put for another night. I know you're only trying to do what's best." She let out a long breath.

"Thank you." He looked instantly relieved. "It really is for the best."

"I know."

"Now let's see what I can do to make sure you get a good night's sleep tonight and not have any more unpleasant dreams. Don't want you waking up halfway through the night tonight."

*****

Bo had left Olivia's apartment an hour before and had stopped in at a 50s diner he had found on his way home to grab a quick bite to eat. The food had been good. Comfort food for a day that had felt particularly long and far harder than necessary. He felt like he did when he came back from a foot patrol in the army. Mentally and physically drained.

He had finished setting up cameras in and around Olivia's apartment, and set up the remote monitoring so he could keep an eye on it from home tonight. He would go back tomorrow to check on things and make sure that no one had tampered with them.

Walking into his sparsely furnished apartment and closing the door behind him, he carefully placed his laptop on the small table in his dining room before heading into his kitchen and brewing himself a pot of coffee. While his coffee brewed, he looked around. There was nothing around that was personal except a single picture of him and his unit from his time in the military sitting on the windowsill.

He walked over and picked it up. Out of the eight men he was pictured with, five had died in combat and two had committed suicide upon return home or shortly there after. The only one other than him still alive was the team leader. A man he no longer spoke to and would probably never again. The rest of the men, his brothers, he missed dearly but that one, he couldn't.

Once he had called that man 'brother', too. He would have done anything that his commander had ordered, but that all changed in one instant when his commander failed him. The man wouldn't listen and it had ended up costing Bo not only half of his unit but also his heart.

And now here he was, back in the same situation once again, and there was absolutely nothing he could do about it. His boss once again was not listening to what he was saying and he was going to have to go through with the mission no matter what. Because that was what a good soldier did. He followed orders without question and completed missions.

No matter how much his mind screamed that this was not the way that it was supposed to be any more, his training took over and he complied. Like a good soldier.

He shook his head.

Placing the picture back on the sill, he went back into the kitchen and poured himself a cup of coffee.

Opening the fridge to get some cream, he realized after looking at the almost empty fridge, that he would have to go and buy some groceries in the near future if he planned on eating any time soon.

Coffee in hand, he sat down at the dining room table and fired up his laptop. A quick system check showed that all of the cameras were operational. He would keep an eye on them for the rest of the night and make sure that no one came near Olivia's apartment without him knowing.

He pulled out her file again; he wanted to learn all he could about her before he next saw her. There was something about her that made him curious. She seemed to have it all, good job, clearly nice apartment but something was missing. Where was her family?

Nowhere in her file could he find anything about family. No mother, father, and the only mention of siblings was a brief mention of a younger brother, but there seemed to be no close contact with him, as he appeared merely as a footnote in the file. Nothing spoke to him about her personality.

He pulled up the cameras on the computer again. He moved their view around the rooms in her apartment. He could see the nice furniture and the fine artwork around the room. There were pillows and throws on the couch, a nice bedspread on the four-poster bed in her bedroom and a hand carved dining room set, but he realized that her apartment was no different than his. She had no personal pictures around anywhere. It was as if she existed solely for her job and then came back home only to sleep.

There was no life there, just things.

He understood that loneliness. Looking at her picture in the file, he wondered what events in her life had caused her to seek out such solitude.

A shrill ringing yanked him out of his thoughts. He reached for his phone.

"Jackson."

"Hey, Bo, how's it going?" Jake's voice came through the phone

"I have all the gear I need set up and working at the

apartment. I will be monitoring it all night long to make sure that the apartment is secure."

There was a pause of dead silence. Bo wondered if the connection had been lost. His apartment was notorious for that.

"Hello?" he said into the phone.

"Yeah, I am here." Jake sounded far away, like he was thinking.

"Okay." What the hell did he want?

"I was actually asking how you were doing. I meant on a personal level, unrelated to the assignment."

"Fine." Great, now Jake was checking up on him. He knew Cat had been wrong about telling Jake how he felt about the situation.

"Well, after our talk earlier today, I just wanted to make sure---"

"I said I am fine, Jake." Bo cut him off. He didn't want to rehash the whole thing all over again. He had already said all that he had wanted to say.

"Alright, alright. No need to get bitchy. It's my job to make sure that the plan goes off without a hitch and it is my job to make sure that all the players have their heads in the game at all times. If I have an idea that there is something that could upset the outcome of the job, I will double and triple check to make sure that we are all on the same page."

As much as he hated to admit it, Jake was right. He had to do what he was doing. Bo would have done no different, had done no different to the men that had been under his command. He just didn't like to be questioned; he was a professional.

"You don't need to worry about me. I will do the job as you have laid out to the best of my abilities."

"Good."

"Was there anything else?" Bo just wanted to get Jake off the phone and get back to the studying of his charge.

"Yes, the reason I called was actually to tell you that Miss Woods will be released in the morning. You will need to pick her up around 9:30."

"Great. I will be there."

"Good."

"Anything else?"

"No. We will talk tomorrow, once you have Miss Woods home and safe," and Jake was gone.

Bo put his phone back down on the table beside him, and rubbed his face with both of his hands. As much as he knew it had been the right thing to do, he was feeling a measure of regret about having told Jake about the misgivings he had about the job. He didn't want his boss, his leader, to have any doubt about him being able to do the job he was tasked with.

He hoped it was the last he would hear on the issue.

Turning back to the file in front of him, he picked up the photograph again. Since he and Olivia seemed to have so much in common, he wondered if she ever felt any of the guilt or regret he did or if she lived a carefree, no-strings-attached.

Chapter 5

Dawn broke shortly before Bo rolled out of bed. The cool morning air drifting in the window brought a chill to his bare chest and legs. He wanted to get in a quick workout session before he had to go pick up his charge. Last thing he wanted to do was have a bunch of pent up energy coupling with his uneasy feeling

He tried to write it off as a side effect of the large amounts of coffee he'd consumed the night before, but he knew better. He had subsisted on coffee for many nights and none of them had left him feeling as jittery as he was this morning.

He stood up stretched and put on a loose pair of track pants. Leaving his bedroom, he made his way across the hall into his makeshift weight room.

Bo caught a glimpse of himself in the wall of mirrors as he walked into the room. He looked like he had been run over by a truck. While he felt like he had rested some last night, it was clear by the lines on his face that he had not rested quite as well as he had thought.

Ignoring the random thoughts about why his sleep was so disturbed, he picked up a set of hand weights and got to work clearing his mind for the day ahead.

Once he had made his way around the makeshift gym in his spare bedroom, he was lathered in fine beads of sweat and his muscles ached. An hour had passed and he had barely noticed. He felt better in his mind, and judging by his sweat-covered image in the mirror, his body was in better shape. Gone were the lines of a poor night's sleep, his eyes no longer looked like he was half asleep, and his well-worked muscles stood out like twisted cables along his lean frame.

He went back into his room, stripped off the now damp sweat pants and walked into this bathroom naked. The hot water soothed the subtle ache in his body and washed away the sweat. There was a part of him that wanted nothing more than to be able to stand there for a while yet and enjoy the hot water. To forget what he had to do that day and take a day to himself.

It was not something he was in the habit of doing, but for once, he wished it was so today.

Taking a deep breath, he shut off the shower and quickly toweled himself dry. Best get at it and get it started. No sense in dragging things out longer than they had to be.

Dressed and packed up, he grabbed a mug of coffee for the road and left his apartment. There wasn't much traffic on the road at that time of the morning; it was still before the rush hour got into full swing. It was the perfect time to make the trip down to the heart of Lake City.

The police had made it sound as if whomever had shot Miss Woods was after her specifically, despite the fact that others at the cafe had been hit and died. So he had to make sure he covered all angles at all times. As he drove, Bo kept an eye on his rearview mirror; it was a habit of his from years gone by when he had to make sure no one was coming up behind him. Today, however, there were so few cars on the road that he didn't have anyone behind him for more than a minute. His mind eased; at least that was one thing that he didn't seem to have to worry about at the moment.

Pulling into the hospital, he spoke to the security guard on duty and asked if there had been any disturbances at the hospital overnight. The guard had only been on duty for a few hours at that point, but he had not heard of anything.

Bo parked his jeep in the same place as he had the day before. The early morning sunshine was still burning off the cold damp of the day before, but the wind had died down to a small breeze.

Crazy weather, Bo thought, and entered the hospital.

The good ole boys from the day before were back again when Bo arrived on Miss Woods' ward.

"Good morning." He smiled; although he really didn't want to get into a long-winded conversation with them at that point, he knew he had best be polite, lest it get back to Jake and that whole grind started up again.

"Well, look, if it isn't the babysitter!" the taller one joked, reaching out a hand to Bo.

Bo cringed inwardly. This wasn't starting off right at all.

"Sorry, man, don't listen to him. He's an ass half the time," the short one responded, smacking the other in the gut.

It was like a horrible comedy scene out of the movies

"No problem." Bo smiled, hoping they would go away and let him be.

"So, you come to pick up her royal highness?" the tall one asked.

"Really? You know she can hear every word we are saying, right?"

Bo watched in amazement. He hadn't had much of an opinion of the two of them to start with, but really, these guys were unreal. No wonder they were stuck having to guard a person instead of solving crimes: they would never get anything done. They reminded him of the Three Stooges, only there were two of them.

"I am here to pick up Miss Woods, that is correct."

"Good luck with that. She has been causing quite the stir this morning." Shorty looked at the tall cop.

"Oh?" Bo asked, eyebrows raised. He had already guessed that the woman would be hard to handle, but he was curious as to just what awaited him.

"They are refusing to release her until you got here. Apparently some sort of doctors ordered that she isn't to leave until her security arrived. She was already a mess last night from what I understand. Caused a bit of a stir until the doc went in and calmed her down."

"Oh, really?"

"Yeah, seems like she wants to get back into her everyday life as soon as possible, even though they still haven't caught the bastards that put her here in the first place."

"Hmm." Bo nodded. This was shaping up to be a little more interesting than he had thought it would be, but also would be far tougher if she was going to insist on going out in public.

"Once you have her in your care, that means the two of us are officially done with our bit for God and country. For this assignment, anyway. It will be all up to you to keep the pretty lady safe," Shorty replied with a grin.

"If she isn't the death of you first," the tall one snickered.

Bo rolled his eyes inwardly. These guys were really cruising for trouble if she really was in the mood they were insisting that she was in.

"Alright then, if that's all you need from me, I shall relieve you of your duties." Bo said, hoping that would be the end of the conversation.

"Good! Get those two out of here so I can go home!" Olivia's voice came from inside the room.

Yes. She was clearly in a great mood. Just great.

The two officers nodded and headed off down the hallway and Bo took a deep breath before he entered the room.

"About time you showed up. I have been waiting for hours for you to get here. And I have had to deal with Cheech and Chong out there making stupid remarks all morning." She was sitting up on the edge of the bed, dressed, arm in a sling and her purse beside her, waiting. "If they think for one moment I haven't been listening to every word that they have been saying, they are sorely mistaken. And if they think that I will not be having a talk with their superiors about their conduct, they are wrong about that as well."

"Good Morning, Miss Woods," Bo said trying to lighten the conversation back up again. He knew the two weren't exactly behaving as they should but really, they were human and being on guard detail day in and day out was not the most wonderful of job to be doing.

"I said you are to call me Olivia. God! Doesn't anyone listen to me anymore?" she huffed and tried to stand up only to drop back down on the edge of the bed again.

"Easy. Take it easy." Bo rushed to her side to make

sure she didn't fall off the bed and hurt herself further.

"I am fine," she snapped, pulling away from him.

Bo pulled back. This was going to be a long day.

*****

She glared at him. She did not want to be stuck in the hospital a moment longer. Not with the two buffoons that they had left as her guard detail again today. She wanted out but the doctor the night before had made sure that she couldn't leave until her security had shown up.

So while she had been up at the crack of dawn and ready to go, she had not been able to even leave her room.

"Let me help you, Olivia. There is no reason to keep going like you are and then you end up hurting yourself all over again."

"Why do you care? You're only here to make sure no one hurts me."

"That would include you not hurting yourself."

"I am not going to hurt myself."

"Clearly you aren't doing yourself any favors when you're busy straining yourself." He reached out to help her up again.

She pushed his hands away, angrily. She didn't want his help. Didn't need it. She was perfectly capable of taking care of herself.

She teetered for a moment trying to bring herself up straight, but lost her balance and sat down hard on the edge of the bed again. A pain shot up in her shoulder and she gasped.

"This is why I am asking you to let me help you, Olivia. You aren't stable on your feet yet. You need to rest."

"I sure as hell am not staying here." He better not think that she was going to stay here any longer just because she had a moment of weakness.

The doctor had said that in the morning she would be able to go home. The night doctor finishing his rounds early in the morning had already said she looked fine, nothing that time and rest couldn't heal, so she was leaving.

"I know you want to go home but--"

"No buts! I *am* going home."

"Yes. Could you please let me finish before you cut me off?" They locked eyes for a moment and Olivia felt her temper flare briefly, but he was right she should let him finish what he had to say.

She said nothing.

"What I was going to say was that while I know you are eager to go home, you have to take it easy or else they might just see you mucking around and change their minds about you being able to handle leaving the hospital." He looked like he was being genuine about what he was saying. "So why don't you let me give you a hand, at least until we get out of here so the nurses and doctors think that at the very least, you are letting me help you and that I will be able to take care of you when they aren't around to hover over you and drive you nuts."

She studied him a moment. He was standing there with hands outstretched to assist her; his face wore a look of honest concern. He did seem like he was trying, but she didn't trust him in the slightest. He could just be trying to lull her into thinking that he was on her side so he could get her to do what he wanted rather than do what she needed to do.

Men were like that. Especially those in charge of protecting people.

He did, however, have a point. She did need his help to get herself out of the hospital. It wouldn't hurt to have him appear to help her. Might make them feel better about letting her out.

"Fine. Only until we get out of here and that's it. I'm not about to let anyone baby me." She knew she sounded ridiculous but she wanted him to know exactly where she stood on the issue. She just needed help out of the hospital then he could go back to being the watchman.

"Fine. You're the boss." He held his hands up in mock surrender before reaching out to her again to help her up.

She allowed him to gently pull her up into a standing position. She teetered a moment on her feet before losing her balance and catching herself on his chest.

She could feel the ripple of muscle beneath his shirt and was close enough to smell the musky smell of his aftershave. Her head spun for a moment, she closed her eyes and she found herself leaning into him, his arms wrapped around her gently, holding her steady.

"Are you alright?" came the low rumble of his voice from above.

She pulled away from him quickly enough to make a pain shoot through her arm. She winced and then immediately hoped he hadn't noticed. She didn't want him to see her hurting.

"Fine. I just lost my balance for a second." She steadied herself again on his arm.

"If you're sure you are alright, I can get a wheelchair, if it would make it easier."

"No, I'll be fine. It was just standing up too fast." After steadying herself, she took a couple shuffling steps towards the door.

She had just about made it out of arm's reach when her world spun again and she felt her legs start to give out. Bo caught her instantly and set her back down on the edge of the bed.

"Maybe I will take that ride." She looked up at him, all the fight gone from her, and smiled meekly.

He smiled back and nodded.

*****

Bo was entirely all too glad that she had finally seen the light and had given up trying to fight the idea of needing help to get out of the hospital. No matter what she wanted, he had a job to do and that was to keep her safe at all costs. And if that meant that he was going to have to keep her safe from her own stubbornness, then that was what he was going to do. She wasn't going to be an easy person persuade, that was one thing that was becoming entirely too clear to him. He was going to have to get creative if he was going to have to be going up against her in order to keep her safe.

He said nothing but picked her up gently and set her

back down again into the wheelchair he had found outside the hospital room door in the hallway. She didn't say a word, but he could tell by how she stiffened when he touched her that she was uncomfortable with the idea of having to be helped with menial tasks. It was going to be a difficult situation for them to get over, as he could tell that she was going to need a lot more help from him in the near future.

"Are you comfortable?" he asked, handing her purse to her once he had gotten her settled.

"As comfortable as one can be, I suppose." There was that glimmer of a smile again and he felt instantly better knowing she was already comfortable.

"Yes. I can't do too much about the comfort level provided by the hospital wheelchairs, but I can tell you that the sooner we get out of here, the sooner we get you into your own home."

"Sounds like a good plan to me." She nodded and he pushed the wheelchair out.

They made their way down the hallway to the nurses' station. Bo wanted to be absolutely sure that the doctors were done with her and that she was, in fact, medically cleared and able to be released. The last thing he wanted was to make it out of he hospital only to have to bring her right back again because they had another test or some such that they needed her for. That was a battle he did not want to have with Olivia.

"Why are we stopping here?" Olivia asked

"I have to be sure that they don't need anything more from you before we get on the road," Bo answered gently, inwardly waiting for her to find fault with his idea and bombard him with protest.

She nodded in silent agreement.

Maybe there was hope for this to work out.

"Hi." He smiled at the nurse on the phone.

She looked up at him and held up a finger as if to say 'hold on one second'.

He nodded and took a step back from the counter; he could wait.

"How can I help you, Sugar?" There was a touch of a

southern drawl in her voice.

"I am going to be taking Miss Woods home and I just want to know if you need her for any testing or anything?"

"I am pretty sure she is good to go home today, but I will have to check her chart to be sure. Give me a couple minutes."

"No problem. We will be here." Bo smiled sweetly.

"Speak for yourself," Olivia mumbled.

"Why do you think you are going somewhere?" Bo raised an eyebrow.

She looked up at him for a moment. He could see by the look in her eyes that she was trying to gauge his seriousness.

He smiled at her and he could see a mischievous glint in her eyes suddenly appear.

"I figured I would head out to the mall for some retail therapy while you stay here and sort this mess out with these ladies. You seem to have it all well in hand."

Bo burst out laughing, and after a brief moment Olivia joined in. Bo didn't know why, but he suddenly felt good about the whole situation. He could feel the tension between them ease some and that gave him almost a sense of relief.

Not that he cared, he reminded himself. This was, after all, just a job for him, nothing more than that.

"Sir?" The nurse's voice snapped him back to reality.

"Yes? I'm sorry?" Bo stumbled over the words.

"She's in the clear to go home." The woman smiled. "But please make sure she rests. She still isn't one hundred percent by any far stretch of the word, so don't let her do too much or she will rip stitches and land herself right back here again."

"Got it," Bo agreed, turning to grab the handles of the wheelchair again. "You hear that, Miss Woods? I don't want any trouble from you."

"The only trouble you are going to have is if you keep insisting on calling me Miss Woods," she replied without missing a beat.

Bo laughed, throwing up his hands in mock defense.

"Now, take me home," she ordered, waving her good hand down the hallway towards the elevators.

"Yes, Ma'am," Bo complied, pushing off in the direction she had pointed to moments before.

"Don't call me ma'am either," she grumbled.

"Yes, Dear," He mumbled back without thinking.

She suddenly turned around in the wheelchair, enough to make him almost loose his grip.

"Don't do that either," she snapped. "We are not, and never will be, friends."

Bo stopped, "I just--"

"No. You are only here because I don't have another choice in the matter. I do not want to get all friendly with you. You won't be around long enough for that anyway." She glared at him, her eyes full of fire.

"Of course," Bo mumbled, feeling instantly like a child being chastised by a teacher.

"Let's go."

He stood there, still reeling from her sudden change in attitude.

"Let's just go already," she said, waving towards the elevators, "I need to get out of here, now."

Bo silently wheeled her into the elevator. He suddenly felt very uncomfortable being in the elevator with her. He wasn't sure what he had done to provoke the shift either.

Leaving the hospital, they said not a word, but Bo could feel the heat of her anger.

Chapter 6

"You're kidding, right?" She laughed as they rolled up beside his Jeep.

"I'm sorry?"

"This is what you drive?" she asked, pointing to his vehicle.

"What is wrong with it?" He looked at his almost decade-old Jeep and wondered what the problem was. Sure, it needed a clearing after the rain the day before had left water spots and splashes of dried road dust.

"Just was not expecting you to drive something like this. That's all."

He looked at her a moment before speaking.

"What exactly were you expecting?"

"I don't know. I guess I was just expecting a bigger, flashier vehicle." She shrugged slightly, "You just seem like that sort of guy to me."

"Flashier, huh?" Bo shook his head. What did she think he was? An ego-filled macho man?

He opened the door to the passenger side and helped her into the seat after some brief struggling.

"Just going to return this to the porters and I will be right back," he told her, closing the door before walking back towards the hospital.

Getting back in the Jeep, he saw that Olivia was holding a picture in her hand. His picture. One of him and the rest of his unit. A candid shot of better days.

"What are you doing with that?" he snapped, snatching the picture back out of her hands.

"I was--" she started.

"Going through my stuff." He felt anger burn through his mind. Just who did she think she was?

She sat there, staring blankly at him, her lips moving but no sounds came out.

"Look, I don't know about where you come from, but where I come from, we don't just start going through peoples things, especially the things that belong to people we don't even know." He waved the picture at her before tucking it back into the sun visor.

"I wasn't trying to be rude," she defended herself, finally finding her voice, "I was just curious."

Bo looked at her. She looked exactly as he had felt just moments before.

"Curious? Then just ask me," he spat, "But then you don't want to be my friend, remember?"

She blinked but said nothing. Bo had to wonder if anyone had ever called her on her own bullshit in her life. Not that he cared, but someone had to tell her.

"I'm sorry, alright?" she apologized quietly, looking down at her hands in her lap.

"Just don't touch my stuff without asking from now on, alright? Or anyone's for that matter," he added, putting the key in the ignition and starting the Jeep.

They pulled out of the hospital parking lot and out onto the road towards Olivia's apartment. The air between them was thick with tension.

Bo didn't understand the woman sitting next to him. One minute, she was joking and laughing. The next, she was biting his head off for doing the same. The very next, she was asking questions to try and get to know him.

"I am truly sorry," she reiterated after a few minutes.

He didn't respond and kept his eye forward and on the road.

"Look, I know I was wrong. I shouldn't have gone through your things." She took an audible breath before continuing, "I saw the picture of your unit and I didn't think. You're right, I was wrong."

Bo nodded but still remained silent.

"And I am sorry for my outburst earlier, too. This whole situation has me rattled beyond anything that I have ever felt before in my life and well, I am afraid. Afraid to let myself get too comfortable with it, lest it becomes the norm for me."

As much as he hated to admit it, he understood exactly what she was going through. With all that he had been through, he too had a hard time allowing himself to get too comfortable in any situation.

It had taken him years to come to accept that his partners at D.O.T. were not going anywhere, and that he could put his faith and trust in them.

He got it.

"I understand that situations like this are never easy to come to terms with," he empathized, looking at her when he stopped at a light.

She nodded and looked out the window. Bo could see tears start to form in the corners of her eyes before she looked away.

"Believe it or not, I understand exactly what you are going through right now," he continued quietly, as the light changed and he drove through the intersection. "I understand the pain and the betrayal. And yes even the fear."

"Ha!" she snorted, "Why would you be afraid? You should have no problem at all protecting yourself."

"You can only protect yourself against what you can see coming. Once you have been caught off guard, ambushed really, you don't ever truly recover from that. You have a hard time relating. So you start jumping at shadows you never would have seen before."

"Is that what it's like to come back from the war?" she asked quietly.

He nodded; his heart was heavy. It was a horrible feeling to never trust again. Most people would never imagine harming another human being, but there was always that one. That one who was lacking something somewhere, that made hurting someone all in the name of furthering their cause. It was that one person that he always felt on guard against. Bo found himself constantly scanning the faces in the crowd, wondering which of the people surrounding him was gong to be that one.

"How long did you serve?" she inquired quietly, breaking into his thoughts as he drove.

"Seven years and six months. Four tours in total."

"That is a lot."

"Some might think that that was not enough for a person like me."

"You were good at what you did?"

"I don't know if 'good' is exactly the word I would have chosen, but certainly we were a unit that went in and did our jobs and did them well."

"What was it you did?" He could hear the prosecutor in her coming out. He didn't want to continue talking about the past but at the same time, he felt compelled to answer her questions all the same.

"Civilian protection. We'd patrol a handful of villages and make sure that no insurgents decided to make one of them a home of some sort or another." He took a breath and pulled into Olivia's underground parking garage. "We gave the peaceful women and children a chance at a normal life."

"That's amazing."

"It was at one time," he responded without thinking and instantly regretted it.

"What do you mean?" The prosecutor hadn't missed a beat; she smelled blood and was going in for the kill.

"It means that not everything turns out the way that it is supposed to." He was short, she had struck a nerve, "I'm sorry, I didn't mean to snap at you. I don't like to talk about it."

"It's alright, I understand." A warm smile crossed her face, " I guess I got caught up in the moment. I'm sorry, too."

The irritation at being questioned quickly evaporated. She hadn't meant it the way it had come across. He could see that.

He parked and helped her to the lobby where the

doorman quickly materialized with a wheelchair. Bo got the feeling he had been standing there, waiting for her to come back since he had gotten in earlier in the day.

"Good to see you looking so well, Miss Woods." The older man smiled warmly, holding he chair steady for her.

"Good Lord, Alfred. We both know I look like hell." A smile stifled as she feigned irritation at the fuss the older man was making.

"Ma'am, regardless, I sure am glad that you are well enough to be released from the hospital."

"Not so sure they let me go because of that; according to this guy, I have to stay put and rest or some such nonsense." She hooked her thumb up at Bo as she spoke.

Bo smiled. He was glad to see that he wasn't the only one she hassled. Maybe this time he would make it through the rest of this assignment.

As much as he hated to admit it, it wasn't quite as bad as he had thought it would be. Maybe Jake had been right all along and this was what he really needed.

Not that he was willing to admit it to anyone.

"Alright, Flyboy. Let's get upstairs before Alfred here decides he needs to team up with you in keeping me stationary. I don't need you both teaming up together."

"Yes, Ma'am." Bo smiled and winked at Alfred as he wheeled the chair towards the elevator and headed upstairs.

Getting off the elevator, Bo watched Olivia scramble to try and find her door keys one-handed.

He pulled up to the door to her apartment and just stood there, watching her fiddle for her keys. She stopped suddenly and heaved a big sigh.

By the time she wiggled around to look at him, he had fished out the keys she had been looking for and was dangling them over her head.

"Looking for these?" Bo grinned.

"Bastard." She grinned back.

"Why thank you, Bo, for keeping my keys safe while I was away," Bo said in a squeaky falsetto, his grin spreading.

Olivia rolled her eyes and tried to reach for the keys.

"Give them to me." She winced as she reached.

"I think you should just leave this part to me, Missy," Bo advised, reaching over her head and unlocking the door and opening it wide enough for the chair to pass through.

"Fine." She rolled her eyes again, waving her hand towards the open door.

*****

The rest of the day had been a delicate dance between what she wanted to do and what she was able to do, and by the time she retired for the evening, Bo found himself exhausted. It had been a long day. He had never realized how difficult it was to care for a single person's every move. As much as she felt better as they day wore on, she still was weak and needed to build up her strength again, so he was left running around to get her whatever she was looking for.

Despite what she had been told, she had gone right back to work on some of her cases almost immediately upon getting in the apartment and getting settled on the couch.

Bo had tried to argue that she should have a nap, but that had been a thought cut off with a single icy look in his direction.

He ordered in Chinese food for them, which she insisted on paying for, but being the gentleman he was, he didn't allow that to happen.

It was around seven in the evening when she had finally given up the ghost and retired to her room for the night. After making her comfortable, he settled in on the couch she had just vacated, with his laptop on the coffee table to keep an eye on the cameras and any alarms he set.

He didn't even realize he had fallen asleep until he smelled the distinct scent and heard sizzle of bacon.

He bolted upright and looked over the back of the couch into the kitchen.

"Good morning, Sunshine." She smiled at him from where she stood in front of the stove.

Bo looked at his watch. Seven thirty. Where the hell had the night gone?

"Morning. How long have you been up?" His mind reeled with the fog of a dead sleep lifting.

She glanced at the clock on the microwave, "'Bout an hour and a half, maybe two hours. I don't know. It was early and you were asleep."

"Why didn't you wake me up?"

"Because you were asleep and it was early?"

"You aren't supposed to be doing that stuff. You are supposed to be in bed resting." He stood up and strode over to where she stood.

She looked at him defiantly.

He reached for the flipper in her hand but quickly found his hand smacked away with it.

"Olivia," he said looked at her.

"Don't give me that look. You are here as my bodyguard. You are not here to be my personal slave."

"Yes, but I am also under orders from--" he started before she cut him off.

"Under orders from whom?" She eyed him.

"The doctor said--"

"I don't give a shit what the doctor said. You aren't being paid by the doctor. You are being paid for by the Lake City Justice Department. I am pretty sure nowhere in your contract is there a clause for waiting on me hand and foot." She put her hand on her hip, still holding the flipper in her bad hand. "And even if there was a clause like that, please believe me, I am not going to allow you to hold me to that in any way, shape or form."

Bo looked at her and he almost burst out laughing. The entire conversation made him wonder if he was in the middle of a dream.

The seriousness in her eyes told him otherwise.

"You may be right. I am not being paid to wait on you hand and foot. But," he held up a finger to silence the protest before it got a chance to make it to her lips. "My mother raised a gentleman and a gentleman would never allow a woman who was hurt or ill to look after herself until she was a hundred percent able to do so."

She stared at him.

"That said, I want you to know that I will not allow for anymore of this foolishness of you cooking breakfast for yourself--"

"I was also making you some," she mumbled, but didn't resist when he pulled the flipper from her hand.

"Very sweet of you, but I think I will be taking over now." He smiled and turned to the stovetop to see to the eggs and bacon she had been making.

She sighed and made her way to the dining room table a few feet away, taking up a position to watch him.

He could feel her eyes watching his every move.

"You look very natural standing in front of a range."

"I spent a good deal of my childhood cooking for my mom and siblings."

"Oh?" She perked up, instantly curious.

"Yeah, my mom was a single mom and raising me and my siblings. She worked a lot of long hours so I ended up doing a lot of cooking for her so she could just relax when she came home."

Olivia smiled at him when he looked at her while he spoke.

"My mother was a single mom, too. But there was just me and my younger brother."

"Two younger sisters and a younger brother. Mind you, we are close in age."

"My brother is seven years younger than me." She looked down at her hands, and Bo wondered what she was thinking about.

"It wasn't easy with all of us being the same age. My mother had to wait a long time to leave my Dad because it was easier to stay and take his shit than it was to leave with four young children to care for."

"Makes sense. My brother was babied badly by my mother. She always felt bad that my father wasn't around to show him how to be a real man." She shook her head but still didn't make eye contact.

Bo said nothing. There really was nothing he could say that would have been non-committal. He didn't want to say anything that could set her off again. He knew how hard it was without a father figure, but the choice was always his to either become a man she could be proud of or not. He had joined the army for that exact reason.

"Sadly, it didn't work out the way she had planned," she sighed. "He decided to take the easy routes in life and I took the harder ones."

Bo still said nothing and just let her talk. Clearly she needed someone to listen to her.

"We don't talk to each other much anymore. Except Christmas when I go home to visit my grandmother." Olivia smiled, "Now, *she* is an amazing person. Always took the time to make sure I had what I needed when my mother was too busy bailing my brother out of whatever he had gotten into."

Bo smiled. He'd had a close relationship with his grandmother growing up, too. The women of that generation were certainly strong, no-fuss women. They knew how to get the job done.

"You know, she was the only one who showed up when I passed the bar?" She scoffed, "My mother was in another city, trying to post bail for my brother. He had been caught running a con and had bilked some old woman out of a few thousand dollars worth of jewelry."

"I was close to my Grams too. She'd whoop my ass if I set one toe out of line and my mother wasn't around to catch it. Hell, she'd whoop me even if my mother did catch it and it warranted a second ass whooping." He laughed, "Man, could she cook a mean meal. She lived down the road from us, and I swear to God, I could smell her cooking from a mile away and it was good. She ended up teaching me a lot of what I know."

It was Olivia's turn to laugh.

"Grandmothers are like that though. They are

wonderful, amazing human beings, born at a time when things weren't perfect but they made it work for their families. And they always wanted to make sure that their kids had better than what they started out life with." She smiled, "And, heaven forbid if you forgot where you came from or what chances you had been given in your lifetime to make a better life. They never let you forget it."

"Nope, they didn't," he agreed, setting two plates of eggs, bacon and toast down at the table in front of her and taking a seat across from her.

"Thank you for this." She smiled around a bite.

"Not a problem. I am just glad you didn't argue too hard about it!"

"Well, if you must know, I was sort of glad you woke up when you did. The grease was getting all splattery and I wasn't sure how I was going to be able to dump it into a can to cool off. Ha!"

"See, I am good for something." He grinned.

They finished the rest of their breakfast in silence, each one enjoying the peace that had befallen them.

*****

Once the dishes were done, Olivia decided that it was time to discuss her plans for the day. She hoped that with his belly full of food and a peaceful conversation, he would be more understanding of how she wanted the rest of the day to go.

She had no wish to spend another day cooped up when she had things she needed to get done.

"So," she started once they had finished eating and Bo was clearing away the dishes and loading them into the dishwasher.

"So?" He turned around, giving her the look that made her think he could read her thoughts.

She hated that look. It was almost as if he was already trying to come up with a way to talk her out of whatever it was she had on her mind.

"Well, I was thinking--" she started.

"From what I have gathered from you, that could be a dangerous proposition."

"Thanks, Flyboy."

"I was in the army, not the air force. Two completely different divisions." He smiled.

She felt her resolve shift slightly. Dammit, why did he always do that? It was so hard to be tough when the guy looked and acted like he did.

"Since I am doing better today--"

"No."

"What do you mean 'no'? You haven't even heard what I was going to say."

"From the sound of how it is starting out, I don't know that I want to hear the rest of it. I figured I would say no before you got too excited about whatever it was."

She stared at him. What the hell! She didn't know whether to be angry at him or burst out laughing. He was certainly a piece of work.

"Give me some credit. I know you aren't going to let me go back to work and do whatever I want. No

matter how much I insist that it needs to be done. I was hoping you would allow me to go into the office and pick up a couple of files that I can work on while I am stuck at home and on bed rest."
She held her breath.

"Are you going to keep doing this to me every day?"

She felt instantly horrible about asking. As much as she hadn't wanted someone to be following her every moment of every day, she had started enjoying Bo's company. It was hard to remember that his primary job wasn't, in fact, to keep her company and make her feel good. It was purely to make sure that she was safe at all times.

From what she had gathered since she had returned home, Bo had set up more than enough surveillance equipment to know what was going to happen before it happened.

Leaving the safety of the cocoon he had built for her would jeopardize her safety and his bottom line.

"Look, I am sorry." She put her hand on his shoulder and felt the ripple of muscles beneath it. "I am not the sort of person who has the ability nor the inclination to sit around and do nothing all day. The fact that I have to is just about driving me nuts. And not knowing when I will be able to return back to the way my life was before this shit started isn't helping."

"I understand completely."

"You do?"

"Of course I do." Bo nodded and got that smile on his face again, the one that instantly melted her heart and resolve, "I know you could have only gotten to the place you are in life with a whole ton of grit and determination. It has become everything you know in your life. It has consumed you to the point where being idle is a foreign feeling and one that you avoid at all costs."

She stared at him. She'd never thought about it that way. Truth be told, now that he pointed it out, she realized that he was right. Her work had consumed her life to this point and she had not left any room in her life to be idle. She hadn't had a hobby or anything like that since she was a child.

"I've never thought about it like that before. I have just been so caught up in it." She looked down at her hands. As much as she hated to admit it, he was right about that.

"I totally understand. I was the same way with the Army. It was hard as hell to come back to the land of the rest of the world when I left active duty. I know I was pretty aimless when I got out too. I suffered from depression along with PSTD." He took a breath, "Hell, I still do. When you devote your life to your job it becomes your life and when that is taken away from you its like you are naked and have no idea what to do with yourself."

"So how did you cope? What did you do?" she asked; she was curious, as he seemed to have it all together.

"I made a conscious decision to make a change. I don't mean the tacky New Year's resolutions that most people make every year. I mean an actual change that required daily changes." He shrugged, "Don't get me wrong. It wasn't as easy as it sounds. My mind fought it all the time. I kept itching to go back to the daily regiment that ruled my life for so many years, but then I'd see myself slipping down that road and I'd get up and go for a run or walk down to the lake or a drive in the country. Something just to break myself out of that head space."

"Sounds like it's just easier not to."

"For sure it is. But if you really want to make the change, then the work you will have to do will be worth it and in the end it will become the new routine."

"I guess you're right." She took a sip of her coffee.

She could feel his eyes on her. She didn't dare look up at him. Didn't want to meet his eyes. It was awkward enough as it was to have him being there giving her a lecture on how to change her life to something that scared her. The whole situation, while it was an eye opener, was not one she was willing to start facing.

"You are still trying to find away to convince me to take you to your office, aren't you?" he said quietly.

She nodded, still not willing to look up and face him.

"Yes."

"Alright, you have been through enough this week to last a lifetime. Now probably isn't the greatest time to change all of your habits. How about a compromise?"

Hope sprung up in her heart.

"Really?" She felt like a kid who had just been offered a chance to earn some extra ice cream after dinner.

Why did he make her feel that way?

"I will take you to your office and we can pick up the files that you want to work on, but I want you to promise me that you will have a nap this afternoon and then take some time to sit back and read a book or watch some television or a movie."
She stared at him. Was he serious?

"I am serious." There he was, reading her mind again.

"Alright. Sounds fair enough to me." She smiled, "Actually it sounds more than fair. I am sure no matter how great I feel right now, I will be needing a nap sooner rather than later."

"Then it's a deal. We both get what we want."

She nodded feeling almost giddy. Why did he make her feel like that?

"Wasn't so hard, was it? I'm not so hard to deal with."

"No you're not at all. As much as I hate to admit it, I am very glad that they sent you to keep an eye on me. I am grateful for the company."

"Me too." He smiled at her and her heart fluttered in response.

Chapter 7

An hour later, after letting her go into her room to get ready to go out, Bo decided to go and check on her to make sure she hadn't hurt herself.

He found her sitting on her bed, halfway dressed, silent tears streaming down her face.

"Olivia!" His heart skipped a beat and he rushed to her side.

"I'm alright," she insisted, pushing him away.

Bo sat down on the bed beside her. He was close enough to smell the faint flowery perfume she had put on. Its smell made him feel momentarily light headed.

"What happened?" he prodded, quietly taking her tiny hand in his.

"Nothing happened." She sniffled. "I just can't do anything for myself and its so frustrating."

"You could ask for help, you know. Like I said, you might not want to treat me like I am some sort of man servant but my momma would not allow me to sit idle while a lady struggles herself into tears." He spoke quietly, and listened as her sobs slowed and eventually subsided.

He had been injured in many a firefight and he knew how frustrating it was to not have the ability to do even the simplest of tasks. He told her as much.

"What, do you know everything about everything?" she asked her big brown eyes looking up into his.

"Not really." He laughed.

"Sure as hell seems like it. You seem to have been through everything I have." She eyed him suspiciously.

"I suppose it does. I just happen to have a lot of experience in shitty situations. Nothing that I can proudly broadcast. However, the way I see it, if I can use some of the shit that has happened to me to help one other person, then it makes the pain and suffering that I may have suffered all the more worth it. If it makes a difference somewhere, it is worth it."

"How the hell are you still so friggin' positive?"

"Like I said, I had a choice: I could sink into the suffering or I could haul ass out of that pit and do something good with my life. Also helps that I have some pretty amazing friends that have been there through a lot of my soul searching shit and pulled me through some of my darker moments." He shrugged, "No man is a mountain. Without them, I might not have made it out."

"You certainly are a hell of a lot different than what I originally pegged you for."

"Yeah, I know you had me as a hot shot, ego-filled flashy-car-driving bad boy," Bo teased, hoping to elicit a smile from her.

"Yeah… about that… I am sorry I laughed at your Jeep. It was quite a comfortable ride."

"She's served me well and I take care of her."

"It shows."

Bo sat there a moment, saying nothing, suddenly very aware of the fact that he was still holding her hand. He could feel the softness of her hand in his roughly calloused hands. He absently stroked it, his mind wandering for a moment to the last time he held a woman's hand.

She gently pulled her hand from his after a moment, snapping him back out of his meandering.

"Do you think you could give me a hand getting dressed?" She turned to look up at him and asked quietly, her voice low.

He could feel her breath on his neck and a shiver went up his spine. He had to give himself a mental shake and answer her question before she thought he was ignoring her.

"Not a problem." His response came out husky and he hoped she didn't notice the change in his voice.

She was an assignment, nothing more. He had to remember that. He couldn't allow what he was starting to feel get in the way of completing the job at hand.

A few moments later, he had managed to help her to get herself dressed and made his way back out to the living room to allow her to finish getting ready. He needed the fresh air more than anything.

The living room felt ten degrees cooler and he found himself almost gulping in the cool air, trying to cool his blood.

It had taken everything in his willpower not to touch her, and when he had, it had been as if he had touched a live wire and a jolt of electricity had flown through his veins. If she felt the same thing, she had done an excellent job of hiding it.

Remember the last time you let your heart get too close to a job? his mind screamed in protest as he walked across the living room to look out the window, *It didn't end well and neither will this. Once this all blows over she will forget you even exist and go back to her life. It will be the same all over again.*

"Youuu whoooo! Bo!" Bo's head snapped around at the sound of Olivia's voice.

"Huh?" he answered, suddenly sounding dumb.

"You looked like you had gone off inside your head."

"Yeah, sort of. Ha-ha," he laughed awkwardly

"If you are done day dreaming, if you could please do me a favor and give me a hand with these running shoes, I would really appreciate it." She held up a pair of battered running shoes.

"Where the hell did these come from?" he asked, helping her into them and tying them up.

"I used to run a lot when I was younger. I keep them around because I have myself convinced that one day I will get back into it again and I will want my favorite shoes when I do."

"Yeah? And how long have you been telling yourself this?"

"I think it's been about seven or eight years now."

"Well done, Miss Olivia." He stood back up and went to reach for the wheelchair.

"I think I am alright to walk on my own," she said, holding up a hand to stop him.

"Oh, this isn't for you, Dear. It's for me. You, girl, are going to run me down. So, I figured you could give me a break for now and push me to the Jeep." He plopped down hard in the chair

Her mouth dropped open for a brief second as her mind caught up.

"You, Mister, need to have your head checked if you think for one hot minute I am pushing your behind anywhere." She put her good hand on her hip and tapped her foot.

"Fiiine." He sighed loudly before peeling himself slowly out of the chair and headed to the door to open it.

She laughed and followed him out the door.

"You know, maybe I should take it with us. Just in case I get tired. " He laughed, going back in for it.

"You aren't serious, are you?" she worried, as he drove it out the door and turned to lock it up behind them.

Bo burst out laughing when he turned around and saw

the look of confusion written on her face.

"Oh, hell no! I just figured if we were done with it for now, we might want to take it back to down to Alfred in case someone else needs it. Or if when we get back you don't feel so great." He shrugged.

"Alright, I know you. You are just looking for a reason to make me push you around in that thing, you sneaky bastard." She poked him in the shoulder as they walked down the hallway to the bank of elevators.

*****

They pulled out into the mid morning sunshine, rolled down the windows and Olivia turned on the radio.

"Am I that bad of a conversationalist that you feel the need to cover it up with the radio?" he joked.

"Oh my god no. I'm sorry!" She instantly turned the radio back off.

"Don't worry, I am just pulling your chain." He turned the radio back on, "Any station in particular that you would like to listen to?"

"Something upbeat. Nothing slow."

"Alright. I think I got something for you." He punched a few buttons and up came one of the college stations, "Dancehall?"

Beenie Man was in the middle of his song, *King of the Dancehall.*

"Really? I haven't listened to this music since I was a kid and my mother played it for us to dance to when we had our family over!" she squealed.

The sound of joy in her voice made him suddenly very happy. Although he really had tried to keep his heart out of the equation, it was becoming more and more evident that he wasn't going to be able to do that.

Bo decided to take the highway across the top of the city to avoid the traffic that tended to clog the downtown arteries.

He glanced over at Olivia. She looked very relaxed, the wind ruffling her hair as they went and a smile playing across her lips.

With all that was going on for the woman, he wished

he could stay on the highway and keep going until the highway ran out, and then race down country back roads to some remote cabin where they could hide away from anyone that would want to do them harm.

Not that it would ever happen, she was a city girl and the city was where she needed to stay.

Bo pulled off the highway and started to make his way south towards the financial district and the courthouse.

He noticed a silver sedan that seemed to be right behind him, mimicking his every turn. The driver of the car stayed back only enough to not draw attention. However, Bo had been followed before and knew the signs. Instead of going straight to the office, he decided to drive around to confirm his suspicions.

He turned sharply onto a side street from the main road. Driving slowly down the street as if looking for a house, he looked back into his rearview mirror. He drove slowly for two minutes and no car turned onto the street with him.

"What the hell are you doing?" Olivia demanded, the concern in her voice evident.
Bo held up a finger to silence her.

He was just about to go onto another street and make his way back to the main road when he saw the silver car go through the intersection ahead of him. The windows of the car were tinted; he could see the outline of the person behind the wheel, but it was too dark to see whether it was a man or a woman who was driving the vehicle.

Bo sat at the intersection for a moment and then hit the gas. He shot through the intersection, trying to get behind the car. He wanted to know who the hell it was. All the other times he had been followed, he had known who was behind the wheel of the car or at least who had hired the person. This time was different.

At the next intersection, he turned right, the same direction the other car had gone; he was lucky that this residential neighborhood had parallel streets. He started to pick up speed, trying to get ahead of the other car. The next chance he had to turn down an intersecting street, he took it, and without slowing down, shot back around and turned sharply onto the street. The silver car was gone. There was no sign of it ahead of him. He kept his foot on the gas, aware that he was going too fast for the neighborhood he was in, praying that there were no children out at this time of day.

He glanced in his rearview mirror again. The silver car was not behind him. He was running out of road as he raced to the end of the street where it had turned off onto another street to avoid the highway. There was still no sign of the silver car anywhere.

He took a deep breath, figuring he had been overreacting and turned back onto main road and looked in the mirror. The silver car was back again.

"Where the hell did he come from?" Bo muttered.

"Are you going to tell me what in the hell is going on?" She was getting more upset by the second.

"Did you notice that car behind us?" Bo said, not bothering to turn around, as he didn't want to give it away to the person who was driving the car that they were aware of their presence.

"Yeah, I saw it on the highway a few miles back but I didn't think anything of it," Olivia admitted, after a quick glance in the rear view mirror.

"I did too, but I didn't think anything of it either. But now I am absolutely sure it is following us. He has to stay closer now because we are in the city core and there is a huge risk of losing us. I am going to try to lose them," Bo decided, continuing to look out the back window through the rearview mirror.
Bo made some tight turns through the streets trying to

get behind the car. There was no license plate on the front of the vehicle so there was nothing he could get to give to the police.

"I want to try and get a better look at who is driving that dammed thing," Bo explained, trying to get a better look at the person who was driving the vehicle and keep his eyes one the road ahead of him. In the glare of the sun on the windshield, it was hard to make out any more than an outline of a person. "Maybe we can lay a trap for --"

"OH MY GOD!" Olivia cried bracing, herself for the impact she knew was coming as the car behind them sped up and rammed the back of the Jeep causing it to fishtail.

Bo gunned the engine after regaining control of the car, trying to put some distance between them and the other car. The car behind them kept gaining on them; they were carrying too much weight to get too far ahead of the other car.

Looking out the back window and bracing for another hit, Bo tried to make out once again who was that was driving the other car.

The silver car closed the distance and once again rammed the back of the now speeding Jeep.

"Turn hard here," Bo muttered to himself, as he turned left and crossed over the other lane of traffic and into a back alley.

The silver car continued on down the same road, completely missing the turn they had made.

After another few quick turns, they were soon headed back in the right direction towards the outskirts of the downtown core and had completely lost the other car. A few minutes later, shaken but unharmed, they pulled into the underground parking lot of the police station, where they both breathed a sigh of relief.

*****

"What the hell was that!" Olivia asked, her brown skin pale and she suddenly looked sick as she got out of the truck and took a deep gulping breath of fresh air

"I am really not sure, to be honest with you but they sure as shit didn't want us to survive that," he declared, getting out the Jeep and walking around to check out the damage.

The rear bumper was mangled and half off, the muffler pipe was bent out of shape, his license plate was missing. There were scratches everywhere.

"I'm sorry about your Jeep. When this is all over, I'll have it repaired." She put her hand on his shoulder.

Electricity hummed through his arm. He gently wrapped his arms around her and pulled her close.

"The company I work for will take care of the damages. It comes with the territory. I am just glad that you are alright. That's what matters to me." He felt her sag against him as he held her. Truly, he was glad she was alright. It could have gone so many different ways.

"Let's go have a talk with Detective Brookshire," Bo suggested, leading the way into the building

They were quickly ushered through security and up to Detective Brookshire's office.

"Detective Brookshire." Bo reached out his hand to shake the detectives.

"Bo, good to see you again, but please call me Stan."
He waved for them to sit in the two chairs sitting in
front of his desk. "Miss Woods, good to see you, as
well. However, as nice as it is to see you both again, I
have a feeling that there isn't anything good you are
here to tell me, based on the looks on your faces."

"Unfortunately, you're right." Bo shook his head, still
trying to wrap his head around what had just
happened in the last hour.

"So, what's happened?"

"Someone just tried to run Bo and me off the road,"
Olivia piped up as Bo gathered his thoughts.

Stan raised his eyebrows and looked at Bo. "This
true?"

"Yeah. Pretty much." Bo shrugged, "When we were on
the highway on the way to Olivia's office, I noticed a
silver sedan that seemed to be mimicking our moves.
When we got off the highway and he followed us
closer, I knew that he was purposely following us."

"It could be a coincidence?"

"Not considering they managed to elude me when I tried pulling around to get behind them and figure out who they were."

"You did what?" The other man's eyebrows went up as he looked between Bo and Olivia.

"Don't. I wanted to try and figure out who the hell it was. The sooner we find out who is behind this, the sooner that Olivia can get back to her life." Bo felt a small flicker of irritation flare up and he had to remember to keep it in check and that the he and detective were on the same side.

"And?" Stan pressed as Detective Trinity entered the room and took up position against the wall beside Stan.

"And the next thing I know, I think I've lost them and then out of no where they show up right behind us and then they proceed to try and run us off the road." "What?" Detective Trinity spoke up. "Run this back again. They followed you, when you tried to follow them back, reverse the roles sort to speak, they got back in behind you and tried to run you off the road."

"Exactly."

"And you didn't think following these guys might be a problem?" The woman's eyes burned holes into his.

"Look, I was just doing what I thought I could do to help."

"Your job is to make sure that Miss Woods' safety is in hand at all times. You are not supposed to be going out of your way to put her life in danger." She crossed her arms, "Just what were you doing out here anyway? Isn't she supposed to be on bed rest?"

"I have a name and I am sitting right here," Olivia piped up before he could get the words out of his mouth. "He was only doing his job. He was protecting me, no matter what happened. And if I may say so, he seems to be doing a far better job than those two that you had sitting outside my hospital room for those first few days."

"I understand your perspective, but you have to understand that he also has to make sure you are protected. He shouldn't even have let you leave the house." The two women squared off.

"Thank you for telling me that I should remain

hostage in my own dammed home. Because that is exactly what people want to do with their lives after they get attacked. Hide away from the world," Olivia fired back.

"You should think about the consequences of your actions instead of being selfish and pigheaded! Your bodyguard could have died or you could have! Or worse, someone else could've gotten caught in the path of one of the cars and was hurt or killed!" Detective Trinity snapped, her eyes full of fire.

Things were quickly going downhill.

"All due respect, Detective, we are both fine, my Jeep will get repaired, and the world hasn't stopped spinning," Bo said, stepping between the women and holding his hands up to settle them down.

"You, Bo, have more balls than I have, stepping between two women like that," Stan complimented, eyeing each of the women.

"Well, they are both out of line so someone had to step in."

"Are you finished, Mr. Jackson?" Detective Trinity

snapped at him.

"Yes, if we can get back to figuring out what the hell happened, and less on what we should have been doing with our day."

"Fine," the detective huffed.

He turned to Olivia.

"Fine with me. The sooner I am done here, the better," Olivia said, clearly done with the situation.

"Good." Stan nodded at them, "Now, did you get a good look at the driver at all?"

"No, the windows were tinted and no matter what angle I was at, I couldn't get more than a silhouette. Could have been male or female, but based on head shape, I am leaning towards male.

"That's a start," Stan said, making notes.

"No license plate on the front and I never managed to get around behind them to see about the back, but I can tell you it was a four door sedan, silver, older model."

"Okay, that should make it somewhat easier to track down. Not too many like that that will have fresh damage to them. I'll have all the body shops in the area notified, and pray that it shows up," Stan said, making more notes. "I'll get the techs to get some samples and pictures of your Jeep. That way, if and when we get the silver car, we have something to compare it to."

"Don't sound so hopeful about the whole thing." Bo sounded more sarcastic than he'd intended.

"What did you expect?" the other detective replied, crossing her arms, clearly still irritated. "You didn't think that we could catch the bastard with that amount of information, did you? You should know better than that. Hell, anyone who watches CSI would know better than that."

"Easy, Jane," Stan said, before Bo had a chance to answer. "Look Bo--"

"Stan, I get it. I will take Olivia home and you guys do what you gotta do to the Jeep." he invited, tossing his keys on Stan's desk.

"Thank you." Stan picked them up, and looked at them a moment before putting them back down, "I will have one of the patrol cars take you guys home."

"Thank you." Olivia was still revved up and Bo knew that the best thing was to pull her out of this and take her home where she could come down from the adrenaline still racing through her system.

"If you guys just want to go back to the main desk, I will send someone to get you sorted out." Stan stood up and waved them towards the door of his office.

They were dismissed.

Chapter 8

Bo was very careful to check each and every corner as they went back upstairs to Olivia's apartment. His nerves were on edge. He didn't like the feeling that someone had gotten the jump on him. He knew the people who were responsible were not done with Olivia and they would stop at nothing to get at her.

It would help him immensely to know what the hell he was looking for, but that wasn't the way that it was going to work for him.

"All clear, Olivia," he announced, and headed to the door of her apartment to open it.

He took a slow step inside. His senses were on fire. He looked around as he stepped further inside. He peered around the corners as he went.

Taking a deep breath, he made his way around the apartment, checking in every closet and behind every door. You could never be too careful, people tended to be very resourceful when they wanted to be. While he hadn't decided whether the people after Olivia were professionals, he was certain that they were determined to see harm come to her.

Sometimes that was worse than any professional: a person who would stop at nothing to see their plan through to the end was a far mightier foe.

He finished clearing the apartment; he found nothing out of place and no sign that someone had been in the apartment since they had left.

Definitely a good sign.

He went back to the door and let Olivia in.

"I didn't see anything that looked out of place." He escorted her into the living room.

"Good. I hope those bastards, whomever they are, haven't found out where I live..."

"Well, they did follow us, so I am assuming that they do know at least the building," he pointed out absently and then when he saw the look on her face he continued, "But I am pretty sure they haven't figured out what floor or apartment. It isn't like there is a directory or anything that they could just walk in and look at. Besides, there is Alfred and the night watchman, both of whom are under orders not to give out any information about you to anyone."

"That doesn't mean dink to me. I deal with assholes like this all the time. Believe me, if they want to know something badly enough, they will find out."

"You're right but with all of the surveillance I have set up, you don't have to worry, we can be on the phone with the PD before they get anywhere near the apartment." He leaned against the back of the couch, "Besides, even if they do make it up here, I have more than enough fire power to hold them off until help arrives."

Olivia looked at him a moment but said nothing.

"I know you probably don't like the idea of weapons being in your house, but the reality is that is what we need to keep you safe and I wont have anything stopping me from doing the job I have to do."

"You're right about the whole gun thing. I don't like the idea, but I agree. For now, it is the best option and

I wont complain about it."

"Good, I am glad that is one thing that we are not going to have to argue about... for now anyway. I would rather not have to think of a different way to ward off the bad guys should they come knocking."

"Just don't get any blood on my carpet, okay?" She laughed nervously and then proceeded to burst into tears.

The adrenaline had finally dropped off and the reality of her situation had sunk in.

"Hey now," Bo said, sitting down beside her on the couch and putting an arm gently around her.

He held her to him and her sobs got harder. Bo didn't know what to say. How did you comfort someone when their reality was that they might not ever get to live a normal life ever again?

What did you say to them to make them feel alright again? There were no words. The only thing Bo could think of was that she didn't deserve to be treated like this. No one did, but especially not her. She had spent her life seeing that justice was done for everyone and here she was fighting to have justice served for her.

Anger swelled up in his veins. It wasn't fair. He wanted nothing more than to go out and hunt the people responsible down. He didn't care for a second what danger that idea held, but he knew that they should pay and pay dearly for what they had done to this innocent woman.
He took a deep breath trying to calm the fire in his veins. Running off all half-cocked would not get him anywhere. It wasn't going to keep Olivia safe and he certainly would become no better than the men hunting her.

Bo held Olivia closer and stroked her hair as she cried. Her perfume was making his head spin again, and it wasn't helping to quell the fires in his blood, but rather shifted their target.

God, what was this woman doing to him.

A few moments later, once her tears had subsided, she pulled away from him.

"Thank you for that," she said, wiping the last of the tears from her face with her shirt sleeve.

"You're welcome. I am just glad I was here for you."

"I am so incredibly frustrated with everything. For the first time in my life, I am actually afraid and I don't like that feeling one bit."

"No one likes to be afraid."

"You know what I mean. I can't stand the fact that I am allowing myself to be afraid. I haven't got time to be afraid of anything." She clenched her good hand in anger as she spoke.

"You are human, Olivia, there is nothing wrong with that whatsoever," Bo said softly. "You know that as well as I do. No matter how you think you should feel, it is what it is. You deserve to allow yourself that release whenever you feel you have to. I certainly am not one to judge you. Nor is anyone else."

She sniffled and nodded and leaned back against the couch cushions.

"I am just grateful that you feel comfortable enough to let your guard down with me. To let me see that you are human and that you are afraid. Not everyone can say that about you."

She looked at him. Their eyes met, and his heart raced.

"I know," she whispered.

The air between them crackled with electricity as they held each other's gaze.

"I think I am going to go have that nap now," she said, quietly getting up.

Bo sat there and watched her walk down the short hallway towards her room. It took every ounce of his willpower to not get up and follow her.

*****

She lay there in bed, still between the nightmare that she had just woken up from and the nightmare that she was living. She let the tears slowly slide down her cheeks. The whole thing had her mind reeling. She had spent the minutes before sleep had taken her, trying to run her mind through any one and everyone that could have enough of a grudge against her want to do her harm.

After all the years that she had spent locking up the scourge that threatened the citizens of Lake City, the list was a long one. No one stood out as being particularly aggressive to her, but then who knew what might have been rolling through the mind of someone she put away years ago. They might have decided to lay the blame for their misery on her feet.

Had one of the cons she put away recently gotten out? No one had warned her that it was happening, but then there were so many it was hard to discern who would be a threat to her life. There were so many.

Why was this happening to her? Why now? What had she done to deserve all of this?

She punched her pillow with her good hand. She was angry and scared. And she was going to do something about this.

Olivia was done being the victim. But how was she going to do anything? She was barely able to dress herself without help, there was no chance that she was going to be able to do anything all on her own.

She needed help.

Bo.

He was going to have to help her. No one else was going to help her. He wasn't going to like the idea, but she was going to tell him in no uncertain terms that he was going to help her to figure out what in hell's name was going on or else she was going to do it all on her own.

He could do his job and protect her or he could sit back and let her do what she needed to get done. There was not going to be any two ways around it. She took a deep breath and slowly sat up and got out of bed.

She took another deep breath and put on what she thought was her best game face. She strode out into the living room, all ready to tell him what she had mentally prepared herself for and instead of being on the couch where she had expected, she found him at the dining room table working away on his laptop.

"Hello there, Sleepyhead. How are you feeling?" He smiled up at her from his chair.

"Bo, we need to talk."

"Uh Oh. Why does that sound like you are about to break up with me?" He feigned concern, "I didn't even know you felt that way about me."

"Bo, I am serious, please listen to me." She pulled out a chair and sat down across from him.

"Alright, you have my full and undivided attention." Bo closed his laptop and clasped his hands on top of it.

"Good."

"So?"

"You aren't going to like this," she started.

"I sort of figured that when you walked out here all serious. I never seem to like it when you are serious like that." He sighed, "So spill your beans. What have you got going on in your melon?"

"I want to try and find out who in the hell is responsible for this."

"What? You can't be serious!"

"I can and I am. I am tired of being the victim. I don't want to hide in the shadows for the rest of my life and I know that they only way that I am going to be able to get out from under all of this is to find the person responsible."

"Olivia, that is why they have the best police detectives in the city taking care of your case. No one in this city wants to see harm come to you. You know that law enforcement takes care of its own. That includes the lawyers and judges that finish the job that they start."

"I know that, Bo, believe me I do. I have full faith in the men and women who are out there doing their jobs to try and help me, and the rest of the city, but please, I hope you can understand that I can't just sit here waiting for them to find the person or persons responsible anymore. I need to do something. I don't want to be hiding away for the rest of my life."

"Olivia, it's only been a few days. These things take time."

"I can't wait any longer, Bo. I am sorry. I have to do something."

"I can't let you do that." He closed his eyes and rubbed

them with the palms of his hands.

She hated seeing him so torn. She knew he was only doing his job but she hoped that he would see the light before she gave him the ultimatum.

"I have to," she said quietly, taking his hand.

Bo opened his eyes and stared directly into hers. His eyes searched hers and she had to wonder if he was trying to see just how serious she was about what she was saying.

"Bo? Please tell me you understand. Please tell me that you will help me. I don't want to do this alone but I will if I have to."

He closed his eyes one more time, took a deep breath and then looked right into her eyes as he spoke.

"I will help you."

Her heart raced, and she had to refrain from jumping up and running around the table to give him a big kiss on the cheek.

"Thank you." She squeezed his hand.

"Don't thank me yet," he said, opening his laptop up. "Come around here and have a look at this."

She got up and walked around the table to sit beside him.

"While you were sleeping, I tried to see if I could get into the cameras down on the streets we were on when that car tried to run us off the road."

"And?" She was instantly hopeful. The images she was seeing on the screen were blurry and she couldn't make out much more than the fact that there were cars speeding down the street.

"Put it this way: I need more help than I have here. I can only see the live feed, which of course, does us no good unless our friends in the silver car are willing to drive back down the same road again." He shook his head, "And even if they were so kind as to drive down it again we would never know the difference between the car that was chasing us and some random look alike car."

"So what are we going to do?" All the hope from moments earlier had suddenly been drained out of her, and she slumped back in her chair.

"We are going to visit my friends down at D.O.T. I know one way or another, they are going to be the ones who can help us identify these people."

"Are you sure?" She was skeptical.

"Only thing we are missing is a vehicle. Then we are good to roll out." He held up his hands.

"I think I can be of assistance there. As long as you don't scratch her up, you can use my girl."

"I would never do harm to a vehicle I am driving." He held up his hand as if to say 'Scout's honor'.

"Yeah right. I have seen you drive, remember?" She headed to the hall to get her shoes and jacket while Bo packed up his gear and got ready to leave the apartment.

*****

The sports car that Olivia drove was almost brand new. He could still smell the leather interior when he got in.

"What year model is this?" He asked, as they got to her parking space.

"2015 edition," she said, smiling proudly as he looked it over.

"Well, you certainly do have a nice taste in cars. Now how about we get in and I will see what this baby can do."

"Again, I feel the need to remind you: please do not mess with my vehicle."

"Don't worry, I am hoping that whomever is behind all of this shit does not decide to come out to play a second time today."

"I hope you are right. I don't know if I can handle any more action of that sort today." Her smiled belittled the emotions that he knew she was feeling.

It had been a rough day and even he with all his years of experience was burned out by the emotional rollercoaster he had been on all day.

The drive over to D.O.T. was thankfully a short and uneventful one. The reception he got when he got in the front door with Olivia at his side was not what he was expecting.

"Bo, what in the hell are you doing here?" Jake came out from behind his desk as Bo and Olivia crossed into the center of the room where the main table sat.

"We need your help," he said shortly, opening his bag and pulling out his laptop.

"Help? Help for what?" Cat's ears perked up as she came out of the weapons room, to see what the commotion was all about.

"I was just about to say. Aren't you supposed to be keeping Miss Woods safe and comfortable at her residence?" Jake asked.

"Yeah, well, after they tried to run us off the road earlier, it has sort of become personal," Bo grumbled powering up his laptop, willing it to go faster as he gave a brief rundown of what happened and where his Jeep was.

"What the hell are you talking about? You were supposed to be at Olivia's home. What the hell were you doing out of it?!"

Bo looked blankly at Jake for a moment. In his mind, he was playing the whole conversation he had had with Olivia earlier over and over. It sounded sad and pathetic. Not something that Jake was going to want to hear.

"It was my fault." Olivia spoke quietly and everyone standing around the table turned to look at her. "I was being a pain in the ass. I wanted to go get some files to work on while I was stuck at home, and I wouldn't leave him alone until he took me. He did try to stop me, but I told him that I was going with or without him. I didn't leave him much of a choice."

"Great. Just fucking great," Jake muttered, throwing his hands up in the air and giving Bo a look that said he was pissed beyond belief.

"Okay, I get it." Bo tried to calm him down.

"Do you?" Jake spat, "Do you really? All due respect, Miss Woods, you don't have a choice in this. Our job is to keep you safe, and the best way we can do that is to keep you in one place with surveillance and let the police do their jobs."

Olivia looked back and forth between the two men, and Cat walked around the table to put an arm around her shoulder.

"I know that it wasn't the best of ideas--" Bo started his mouth suddenly dry.

"It wasn't the best of ideas, Bo? It was an absolutely horrible idea! And to make it worse, you both could have been killed! What the hell were you thinking, man?"

Bo said nothing.

"I know you did not want this assignment in the first place but for crying out loud. I thought you, of all people, given everything that happened, would have been able to keep her safe."

"That's not fair!" Cat interjected, trying to usher Olivia into another room away from the storm that brewing.

"No, Cat, it's true! I expect that he would be one that would throw his all into seeing that she was protected. It was supposed be a chance to make shit right in his mind again. Instead I end up with someone who acts like he is green and never done a protection detail in his life!" Jake was mad.

"Jake, that is enough." Bo's own anger starting to spill over, "I know that it was a mistake--"

"A mistake that almost cost you everything, *again*."

"No! It was never going to be that again--"

"And just how in the hell can you be so sure of that? Look at the last time! You had it all under control, until your CO took the control away and then what? It was no different than today."

Bo's heart ached. Why was Jake bringing all of this shit up now? Bo had enough to worry about and besides this entire thing was Jake's idea in the first place.

"You need to pack your shit up and head back to Miss Woods' apartment. Now. No more bullshit, Bo," Jake ordered, turning and walking away, "I am going to head over to the police department to see what they have done with your Jeep."

Jake grabbed his jacket and stormed out of the office.

Chapter 9

"He was way out of line," Cat said, coming back into the room as Jake left.

"He was right."

"No, he wasn't. What happened overseas? You couldn't do anything about it. You couldn't save her even if you had tried. If anything, you could have lost your own life in the process."

"He was right though, I still shouldn't have allowed Olivia to put herself in danger." He rubbed his hands with his face. What the hell had he been thinking?

"You didn't have a choice, Bo."

Olivia stepped out of the room she had been taken to. "Forgive me for not staying in one place. I meant what I said. You had little to no choice but to accompany me to the office. I would have taken a cab had you not gone with me. And that would have been a complete disaster. If you had not been the one driving the vehicle, I was in there is no chance in hell that I would have survived."

"You have a point, Bo is an amazing driver." Cat nodded

"So please stop beating yourself up. I will have a talk with Jake about all of this when things are said and done and see what I can do to help cool his head off." Olivia put a hand on his shoulder and Bo saw the expression on Cat's face when she did that. A mixture of shock and a smile

What was Cat thinking? That he was sleeping with her?

He wasn't. She was an assignment. He pulled away from Olivia's touch.

"Alright. You came here for help. What did you want help with?" Cat asked, breaking Bo out of his thoughts and back onto the task.

"For one, I managed to get into the city servers to view the live feed for the cameras on the streets that I was on when the bastards started trying to do their thing-"

"Someone was paying attention when I was teaching them," Rudy interjected, smiling, coming up beside the three of them. "Pleased to meet you, Miss Woods, I'm Rudy, the resident tech guy."

"Olivia, please," Olivia said, taking the hand he held out to shake.

"So, you got into the city cameras, great lesson, and?"

"Yeah, it was a great lesson you taught, however, there is only one problem."

"What's that?" Rudy said watching the images of cars whiz by on the camera.

"Unless our friends are going to come by and wave at the camera, we need to see the archives of the footage from earlier today."

"Oh, right, duh." Rudy shook his head quickly.

"Can you help us?" Bo could hear the hopefulness in Olivia's voice.

"I can, but I have to ask what the hell are you going to

do if I can dig up the footage."

Bo and Olivia looked at each other. Bo hadn't really thought that far ahead, he was grasping at straws.

"I had this idea that if I was able to see the footage, I might be able to get a license plate that the police could track down," Bo said, shrugging his shoulders.

"That sounds logical, but you know you could have just given me a call to do that for you and you would have avoided that whole showdown with Jake." Rudy walked back over to his bank of computer screens at the back of the room.

"Yeah, well... I wasn't expecting Jake to behave quite like that," Bo explained, trailing after him.

Both Cat and Olivia followed until they had all crowded their way into the back corner of the office around Rudy's desk.

"No pressure or anything," Rudy muttered, as his fingers flew across the keyboard.

Bo watched in fascination as Rudy expertly navigated his way through all of the different screens; streams of codes rolled up the screen as he went along. Bo always wondered how Rudy could keep track of everything that he was typing at the speed he was, but then from what Bo understood of Rudy's past, while he was young he had been doing this for a very long time.

He once managed to hack into the computers that run all the street lights and turned them all red remotely. The city had ground to a halt for almost a half an hour while they worked to undo what he had done.

"Go it." Rudy smiled as the code slowed down and a pop up with files came up.

"What am I looking at?"

"You, my well-muscled friend, are looking at one hour bites of the traffic cams across the city. What were the streets and times again?"

Bo relayed the information Rudy needed and a few more keystrokes and clicks later, Rudy stopped again.

"I think this is what you are looking for."

On the screen was a screen shot of the back end of the silver car that had been chasing them. Smack in the middle of the screen was a crystal clear shot of the license plate.

"How the hell did you do that?" Cat's eyes were wide.

"If you paid attention more when I am showing you things, then you would have a better understanding of how I do these things." Rudy rolled his eyes.

His computer beeped. Another pop up appeared.

"And there we go. Hang on, I'll print it out for you."

"What the hell?"

"I had it run the plate while you all were oogling the fact that I managed to find the shot of the license plate."

"Brilliant." Bo smiled.

"Also sent off a package to Detective Brookshire, so he now has all of this information. I do hope it helps. At least helps you enough that you both can go back to Miss Wood's place and not get yourself into any more mischief."

"Thanks for that," Bo said, taking the sheet from Rudy's printer.

"Any time."

"Does this name mean anything to you?" Bo asked, handing the piece of paper to her.

Olivia looked at it a moment and Bo could see the look of shock and horror pass across her face.

"What is it?" Bo asked instantly worried again.

"This is my brother," Olivia said, holding up the page in good hand.

"Your brother?" Bo felt his heart hammer hard in his chest. "Why?"

"Yes, my brother." Olivia struggled with the words, Bo wanted so much to reach out and hold her. Nothing was worse than having to find out that a family member might be the one who tried to kill you.

"What can you tell us about him?"

"I haven't seen him in seven or eight years now, I

guess. He was into some pretty heavy shit the last time we spoke. I didn't get all of the details, being an attorney for the justice department, but you know how that goes. I figured I would one day have to be removed from a case that involved him and some sort of wrongdoing. I never imagined any of this." She gestured to her arm in the sling, tears filling her eyes.

"I don't think any of us would think that our family could do us harm," Cat empathized quietly.

"The good news is that the police now have a lead on him and if there is any merit to him being a part of this then they will have him in custody soon enough and we can sort this out." Rudy looked down at his keyboard.

"I think I want to go home now," Olivia said quietly.

*****

They pulled out into the late evening night. The darkness in the industrial area was punctuated by the occasional streetlight.

Her head was swimming with thoughts. How was her brother related to all of this? What was he doing?

She knew they were right. That there was nothing more that she could do about the situation. She felt badly. Someone else who had been shot that day at the cafe had not made it and it was all because of her and her bother.

Bo hadn't said anything since they had gotten in the car. She wondered what he was thinking as she glanced over at him.

"I'm sorry," she said quietly.

"For what?" Bo asked without taking his eyes off the road.

"For all of this. Getting you into trouble with your boss and now this whole mess with my brother." She felt the tears welling up in her eyes again.

"Don't be, Liv, it's not your fault." The sound of his voice, as he spoke, the way he shortened her name, something no one had done for years, sent shivers down her spine.

"I just don't understand any of it. I don't know why Gerald would want to hurt me. I haven't done anything to him. I just have left him to his own devices."

"That was probably the best thing you did for yourself but it may have also been the thing that's been festering at him all of these years. Guys like him don't like seeing other people succeed. And you have succeeded far beyond what you should have given the rough start to life."

She said nothing, he was right. It wasn't what she had done to him, but rather what she hadn't done. She hadn't been there for him, hadn't helped him to see the light of the good side of life. She had left him to rot while she blossomed.
"You are alright. Sometimes people like that can't be fixed. They don't want to be. They think that what they are doing in life is what they were meant to be doing. That it is somehow alright and that there isn't any other option out there for them. You can't change a person who doesn't want to even see that there is a problem or that what they are doing is wrong."

She could hear a twang of pain in the last words he spoke.

"I am sorry about dragging you into this mess. And

what happened with Jake. I really shouldn't have forced you to break the rules in order to make me happy. It wasn't fair."

Bo stopped at a stop sign on an empty street, not a car nor a person was around, and looked right at her.

"Olivia, I don't do anything that I don't want to do. I learned a long time ago that sometimes you have to go with your gut instinct and not the orders on the paper. The orders on the paper are not always right. They don't always make sense and if you think even for a second that there is something amiss or wrong or something that could be done differently and have a better outcome you have to go with that feeling."

"But you were in the army. Aren't you supposed to follow orders, no matter what you think?" She searched his eyes in the dim light.

"Yes. We are supposed to. But even those orders aren't always ones that make sense and people can get hurt," he said, looking away and putting the car into drive again before heading left down the street.

They drove along in silence. Olivia mulled over what he had said.

"Who was she?" she asked and then almost instantly regretted it. It wasn't her business but she had asked, she only hoped that he wouldn't be mad at her.

Bo said nothing for a bit but kept his eyes squarely on the road.

"Her name was Sooraj. Her name means *Sun in Urdu.* And she was my ray of sunshine. She was a villager in one of the villages that we were set to protect. It happened by accident. One day, I was on patrol and she came up to me with food and water. They were always doing that for us. It was their way of showing us their gratitude for what we were doing for them.

We sat and talked while I ate, and the next day it was the same. Every day we would eat together. I found myself eagerly awaiting the time when I knew I would be able to see her again.

I never expected it to go as far as it did, but I found myself helplessly in love with her. I was so much in love that once I was done with my tour that time, I was going to retire from the army and find a way to bring her home. Settle down and start a family. "

Olivia nodded. "What happened? Why didn't you?"

"About a month after we started seeing each other, word came down that the village she lived in was in reality a base of operations for some insurgents. That they were building bombs and IEDs there. I told my CO that there was no way that was true, as I had seen nothing but innocents in all of my time there. But he wouldn't listen to me. They raided the village that night and killed nearly everyone in it. It was only after the fact that they realized that their information was tainted."

Olivia's heart ached as he told the story. She could hear the pain in his voice as he spoke. He had really loved her.

They didn't say another word for the rest of the ride home. The night watchman tipped his hat to them as they waited for the elevator to take them upstairs.

"I am so sorry, Bo," she whispered as they got onto the elevator.

"Don't be. It wasn't you."

"I shouldn't have pried like that. It wasn't fair or

right." She had felt incredibly horrible about the whole thing.

He stepped out of the elevator and onto her floor, taking careful, measured steps down the hallway, checking and rechecking to make sure everything was clear.

He went into the apartment and came back a few moments later.

"All clear." And ushered her in.

He sat down on the couch and breathed a heavy sigh before turning to set up his laptop once again. She turned and went to her liquor cabinet. It had been a long day.

"Do you think that's a good idea with the pain meds you are on?" Bo questioned, watching her pour two glasses of an amber liquid.

"I don't give a shit at this point. I have had a really horrible day and I need something to take the edge off." She sipped and handed him a glass as she sad down on the couch beside him.

He looked at it a moment before accepting it.

"It's my way of saying I'm sorry for all the shit that's happened," she explained quietly, leaning her head on his chest.

"I have already told you that I don't do anything I don't want to." His voice came out as more of a rumble and she felt that all too familiar shiver run down her spine.

*****

Olivia looked up at him. Their eyes met for the briefest of seconds before he leaned in towards her.

His lips were warm and soft, and Olivia felt her head spinning with growing arousal as she felt the tip of his tongue against her lips, gently parting them, then slowly moving inside her mouth to meet her tongue passionately.

She couldn't quite tell how long the kiss lasted, but she knew wasn't as long as she would have liked. Bo pulled away just enough to look into her eyes and smile.

Olivia smiled back, although she ached for more of his touch. She wanted to feel his lips again... she wanted to feel his hands, his fingers, his every body part against hers.
And she could have him, if she wanted him, Olivia realized. And she did want him. She wanted him more than anything.

"I want... you," she whispered to him.

He kissed her softly, and declared, "I am yours."

She swallowed, his deep words sending shockwaves of excitement through her.

"I want you... to touch me," Olivia told him, her voice suddenly unsteady.

He obeyed, and lifted his hand to her face, slowly tracing it with the tips of his fingers. Olivia shivered, closing her eyes as he continued to caress her face, then moved on to clasp the back of her neck.

His hands came back up, slipping the material away to cup her warm, full mounds.

"Oh... " she groaned.

She wanted this, this slow and tender exploration. One by one, each piece of her clothing, as if by magic, disappeared.

She was naked now, naked for the first time before this man.

"You are so beautiful," he whispered.

"Bo..." she trembled. But he was already gathering her in his arms, lowering her to the bed.

When he had made sure she was lying comfortably, Bo lay next to her, and she noted with a bit of disappointment he was still fully dressed. Well, she could take care of that.

"Wait," she said, as his hand reached for her.

"I want to see you, too. Take your shirt off."

He smiled coyly, reaching behind his head too slowly -- much too slowly, and slipped his shirt off over his head. The ripples in his chest were now exposed to her adoring gaze; she stared at him hungrily.

Somehow, she found him different than she expected, not as bulky as she had imagined this man to be, but he did have a well-defined muscular trimness and a sensuous grace about him she found to be much better than what she had expected.

She very much wanted to touch and kiss his newly exposed skin, but again she resisted. For some strange reason, she was enjoying remaining passive, and she lay back to allow him to continue. But wait, there was just one more thing...
"Wait, Bo-- your hair. I want you to take your hair down."

She watched with excitement as he flipped his dreads over his shoulders. They were longer than she had thought they were.

He took her right nipple between gentle fingers, rubbing it slowly, making her moan and close her eyes. Olivia threw her head back, exposing her neck, and she felt him leaning closer to her to kiss it, running his tongue along her jaw. The ends of his thin dreads brushed against her skin, tickling it as his lips gently tickled the lobe of her ear.

Olivia shuddered with another tingle of pleasure when she felt the tip of his tongue against the swell of her nipple. Bo circled it a few times, then closed his lips around it, suckling gently. His teeth then closed around it, and she squirmed, grasping the back of his neck in silent ecstasy.

His lips never leaving her skin, he moved on to her other hardened nipple and took it in his mouth, repeating the same delightful ritual he had done to the other one.

She pushed her hips upward and spread her legs, waiting as his lips caressed her stomach, her abdomen, trailing their way down her body with excruciating slowness to where she wanted him the most. She was already more aroused than she would have thought possible, every precise movement of his mouth sent shivers to every part of her.

His fingers stroked the tender insides of her thighs, moving up until he was nearly touching the patch of hair, but always pulling away before making actual contact. She groaned in frustration, but he didn't tease her for long.

She found his eyes again, and her mouth parted in a silent plea. He answered it by leaning towards her, engulfing her in a strong, passionate kiss.

The corners of her mouth curled into a smile; he tasted so good, his skilled lips felt so soft; she would have been content to lie in his arms and savour him forever.

Bo's fingers gently felt within her soft feminine folds for her moist opening. It flowered open at his touch, and Olivia's eyes closed in ecstasy as his fingertips gently rubbed around it. If she could have formed any words, she would have begged him not to stop, to keep touching, but she didn't even have to. He quickly rubbed and then pinched the sensitive little bud that brought her so much pleasure, making her stretch her body sensuously in complete abandon.

Yes! Oh, yes... so close...

But then his fingers left her, and Olivia barely had time to return from the edge of her abandon when she felt warm breath and then the moist softness of his tongue now against her. She cried out in pure delight as he gently lapped at her.

Yes... yes... ! her mind screamed.

"Don't... stop!" she gasped, and could barely manage a cry as his firm hands held onto her thighs and the hot moisture of his tongue darted out to caress her with a stronger insistence, lapping at her until that remarkable pleasure climbed again and peaked.

"Oh... yes!!"

Her body arched, her head kicked back and a long cry escaped her lips as the most incredible climax firmly gripped her, rolling through her like fierce waves. For that short time, it consumed her and became her entire world.

Chapter 10

Bo lay there in bed beside her as the early morning light filtered through the sheer curtains on the window. He watched as the sunbeams played across Olivia's ucovered leg. She was magnificent and beautiful.

She was so incredibly strong, she had faced everything that had been thrown at her in the last few days and had not run and hid. This woman was a force to be reckoned with.

He gently, idly stroked her bare shoulder, inhaling deep breaths of the woman lying in his arms.

"Penny for your thoughts," she whispered, as she reached out with her good hand to stroke his cheek.

"Just admiring the beauty that lies beside me." He smiled and leaned down to kiss her nose.

"Why, thank you. I'm a bit of a hot mess at the moment." She smiled and gingerly raised her bad arm.

"That didn't seem to stop you last night," he chuckled.

"Someone made it hard to resist." A gentle smile played on her lips.

He wanted nothing more than to wrap her in his arms and hold her tight. He never wanted to let her go. She brought back all of the feelings he thought were dead in him and that was something that he would never let go of again.

In the last few years, he had never felt so alive as he did at that moment.

"Where does this go from here?" she whispered.

He said nothing, holding his breath. Did she think that he was going to leave her? Or was she trying to find a way to wiggle out of what had occurred between them? Was she having second thoughts?

Panic welled up in his throat

"Wherever you want it to go." His voice shook a bit as he spoke.

She rolled over to look at him.

"What is the matter?" Her eyes searched his. He could see the same fear in hers as he felt in his own heart.

"Nothing. I just am not sure that I am what you want."

"What do you mean? What is so wrong that I wouldn't?"

Bo sighed hard and fell back on the bed. There was too much for him to list.

"My job for one. It is not easy. You yourself have seen what can happen in a blink of an eye."

"I also saw how you handled the situations. I know if anyone can get through that stuff, it's you." She placed her head on his chest.

"But what will happened if one day I don't come home?"

"We will cross that bridge when we come to it."

Bo's heart eased, and he started breathing deeply. She wanted to give this whole thing a try. She didn't want to let the entire thing go down the drain. He might actually finally have a chance at a normal life.

She snuggled in deeper into his chest and he tightened his arms around her. For the first time in a long time, he felt really at peace with the world. He knew that they were still in danger but he also knew that somehow it would all work out in the wash.

He just had to believe that it would. He kissed the top of her head and closed his eyes.

*****

He had just drifted off into a light doze with his arms wrapped around Olivia, when there was a crash, as Bo heard the door to the apartment fly back on its hinges.

Olivia stifled a scream as Bo jumped out of bed and reached for his clothes. His gun lay nestled in the folds of the fabric and it took precious seconds to pull it out. Olivia quickly ducked to the floor beside the bed as far away from the door as she could get.

"Olivia!" A mans voice hollered down the hallway. "Come out! I know you're back there! There is no use hiding anymore."

Bo said nothing but motioned to Olivia to stay quiet. She nodded and hunkered down as far as she could. Bo made his way along the floor as low to the ground as he could.

"Olivia!" the man called again, "What is the matter? Don't want to come and see your brother anymore?"

Her brother. Great. This was not going to go well. No where near how he had hoped that this would all play out.

Bo edged his way closer to the doorway around the closet. He peered around the corner quickly and he could make out the figure just around the corner of the front hall. Thirty feet away.

There was nothing in between them. No where for her brother to hide if he chose to come out from around the corner. Bo would have a clean shot. Not that he wanted to take that shot but he would not hesitate if the man came down the hall with the intention of doing Olivia harm.

"Olivia! You need to come out so we can talk about this like rational human beings."

"Go away, Gerald! I don't want to talk to you!" Olivia's voice came from behind him, strong as ever.

What was she doing? Bo glanced back at her and signaled for her to be quiet.

"For a second there, I was wondering if I had gotten the apartment wrong and this wasn't yours!" The voice sounded closer. Bo took a quick peek around the corner and saw that Gerald had come out from his hiding spot and was making his way down the hallway slowly towards the room.

Bo fired a shot, wide on purpose and it lodged in the wall a few feet from Gerald's head. Gerald scurried backwards and ducked into the living room.

"Oh! I see your little boy toy has some balls on him, does he? Does he really think that he is going to be able to protect you?"

Bo listened, trying to get a bead on where in the rest of the apartment he might have gone. He couldn't quite get it.

Almost as if she had read his mind, Olivia spoke up again.

"He is far more of a man than you will ever be, Gerald." There was bitter venom in her voice as she spoke.

"I don't know about that. But he certainly is a poor shot."

Bo just listened.

"What I don't understand, Gerald, is why you are doing this. I haven't done anything to you."

There was silence.

Bo strained to hear what the man might be doing.

"Is that what you really think?" He finally spoke, sounding further away.

"What have I ever done to you that would ever warrant this sort of treatment?"

Gerald laughed.

"You don't get it, do you? You wouldn't though. You are perfect. You are everything that I am not. You went to law school and I--"

"That was your choice, Gerald. I had nothing to do with your choice. I made mine and you made yours."

"But everyone loved you. You were the perfect one."

"I never did anything to you or your life, Gerald. I stayed away and left you to handle your own business."

"Do you know where that got me? Multiple jail terms, Olivia. And do you know I called and I wrote and I tried to get you to come and help me and nothing. My big sister was too dammed busy living her high and mighty life to be bothered to come and bail her little brother out. Do you know how many times I was the fall guy for someone else's shit because they thought I was going to have my big sister to help get me off?"

Bo looked at Olivia. He could see the torment in her eyes. There was a part of him that wished that the man would just shut up and stop torturing her. Just do what he came here to do and leave.

"I couldn't do that even if I wanted to, Gerald. You know I have to follow the law to the letter. I can't do anything that would be considered against the law. Not for anyone."

Olivia had moved closer to Bo as she spoke.

"Maybe I can talk him out of this," she whispered to Bo the second she was close enough. "It's my fault we are in this mess, I have to see if I can talk him down. He is my brother."

Bo shook his head hard but she wasn't listening anymore and was slowly making her way towards the open bedroom door.

"What are you doing," Bo hissed, "Don't go anywhere."

He tried to reach for her but she was already to the door, looking tiny in the oversized t-shirt.

"Gerald. Let me come out there and we can talk about this. Together. Maybe we can find a way to work this out and put and end to it."

She took a step towards the doorway with her hands raised in surrender.

Bo felt his heart jump into his chest. He wanted to run to her and pull her back out of the way of danger but he also trusted her and knew that if anyone could talk him down it would be her.
"You are looking pretty good," Gerald observed. "For some one who was shot a few days ago."

"I am still in a lot of pain but I forgive you, Gerald. I know you didn't mean to hurt me."

Bo heard the distinct click of a gun being cocked. His heart hammered in his chest.

"Actually, sweet sister of mine, I did. You see, my friends think that somehow you are behind a lot of their troubles. You have been busy putting a bunch of them away for a very long time. Now because you are so good at what you do, they think that I am in some way helping you get the information that you need to prosecute the cases you do. They don't think that you and the rest of the police are smart enough to do all of the work on your own."

"I--" Olivia started

"I know you would never help me, nor I help you. But my friends, they don't believe that. And the only way that I can prove it to them is to kill you myself. It seemed like a fair trade. My life for yours."

Bo slowly stood up and peeked around the corner and he could see Olivia standing at the mouth of the living room her hands still raised.

"And here you are all nice and neat in front of me. Or did you still think that you would be able to talk me out of it?" The gun clicked again.

Bo couldn't wait any longer; he dove out of the room headed straight for Olivia. He grabbed Olivia, pushing her to the ground, behind the couch as he fired off shots in the general direction of where he thought Gerald would be as he went.

Gerald, too, fired back. Bo had missed him somehow.

Just then, the busted front door flew back on its hinges once more.

"FREEZE! LAKE CITY POLICE DEPARTMENT!"

Men in full SWAT gear stormed into the room.

"DROP YOUR WEAPON, MISTER WOODS AND KICK IT TOWARDS US."

There was a clatter as the gun fell to the floor.

Bo could hear Olivia sobbing as she hid under his chest. He pulled her close.

"Shh. It's going to be alright now. Everything is going to be alright." He kissed the top of her head.

*****

"How the hell did you know?" Bo asked Stan as soon as he found him, once he was sure Olivia was in good hands with the paramedics the police had brought with them.

"Actually, it was your pal, Rudy that really helped us out. The package he sent me last night gave us all the information we needed to get a search warrant for Gerald Woods' place of residence."

"I take it you didn't find him sleeping in bed?" Bo raised an eyebrow.

"No, we did find a whole ton of information on Miss Woods and her habits and such. We knew we had the right guy, but we didn't have a clue where to find him or what he was planning for his next move."

Bo nodded.

"I was just about to come over and have a talk with Miss woods and you about the situation when I found him sneaking in the back door of the building. So, I made a quick call and here we are." Stan gestured around the room.

Techs were busy taking samples from here and there. One of the techs had his laptop and was looking through his surveillance equipment and files.

"From what he said to Olivia, he was here purely to kill her off as he is involved in one of the gangs that Liv has been cleaning house on lately and the gang members think that he is the one feeding her information. So they told him to prove loyalty to the gang and kill her."

"That's lovely. Total show of brotherly love." Stan shook his head

"Yeah, apparently the two haven't spoken in the better part of a decade. So there is no way in hell that he was helping her at all."

"Gangs don't see that. They only see whatever it is that they want to see."

"Exactly. For Gerald it was either he dies or Olivia does. There was no in between for him." Bo shook his head. So much waste. If he had succeeded, there was no guarantee that he would have been spared by the gang. They very well might have killed him anyway.

Bo said as much to Stan.

"You're absolutely right. At least now the poor bastard stands a chance to live to see another day. We will keep him segregated from the general population until we get things sorted out. Might see if I can't flip him and get him playing for our team for real this time."

Bo nodded and turned to walk over to where Olivia was being checked out.

"And one other thing," Stan added, stopping him in his tracks. "I am not going to say anything to Jake about your current attire, but I think, you should tell him yourself."

Bo looked down at his loose fitting track pants and suddenly felt very exposed. Stan had him dead to rights but he was grateful for the other man's silence. Bo would have a talk with Jake once this whole mess blew over and things went back to normal.

"Thank you."

"You're welcome and good job," Stan praised, reaching out a hand for Bo to shake.

Bo headed back over to Olivia.

"How are you doing?" He could see a fresh bandage had been place over her wound but it was slowly filling up with blood.

"Tore my stitches open when you pushed me to the ground." She winced.

"I am sorry about that. But I didn't have --"

"I know you didn't do it on purpose. You were only trying to save my life, which might I add, you succeeded in doing." She smiled at him.

He sighed and wrapped his arms around her. All was forgiven. For that split second everything was suddenly right in the world. In his mind's eye, he could see Sooraj's face. She was smiling, happy even. She too, had forgiven him.

Tears came to his eyes. He buried his face into Olivia's hair.

"Thank you, Liv," he whispered into her hair.

"Thank you, Bo," she whispered back.

He held her tight and promised himself he would never let her go.

Made in the USA
Charleston, SC
23 March 2016